HAIR
IN ALL THE
WRONG
PLACES

ANDREW BUCKLEY

Month9Books

Published by Tantrum Books for Month9Books, Raleigh, NC 27609
Cover illustration by Zachary Schoenbaum
Cover design by Najla Qamber Designs

For hairy teenage werewolves everywhere …
… you're not alone.

HAIR

IN ALL THE
WRONG
PLACES

A WARNING TO THE CURIOUS

I don't want to get too scientific here, but there are a few things you should know before you sink your teeth into this book. Werewolves were everywhere in Europe in the late sixteenth century. Go to a party, there would be a werewolf. Go to work, you're probably working next to a werewolf. Bump into a stranger on the street—werewolf!

But the true nature of a werewolf is a terribly hard thing to control. Eventually you get that urge to eat someone. And let's face it; eating people is just rude. Fast-forward to today, and you hardly ever see a werewolf anymore.

Now here's the scary bit, the bit that concerns *you*. Yeah you, reading this book! Come closer. This is important.

While werewolves ceased to be a part of the world, they didn't necessarily leave it. On the contrary, humans evolved to repress the werewolf gene out of the fear they would be decapitated, shot with a silver bullet, burned alive, or a terrifying combination of all three. What this means is that every single human being is still carrying the werewolf gene. You, right now, sitting right where you are, have the werewolf gene swimming around somewhere inside of you.

It's just not active. Not yet.

To fully activate that werewolf gene, you'd have to be bitten by another werewolf, someone who turns into a giant wolf-like creature when there's a full moon. So fear not! As long as no one has bitten you recently, you're probably okay.

So why this warning? You're probably thinking there's no chance I'll turn into a werewolf because I haven't been bitten. That is absolutely true. However, it is very possible to awaken the sleeping werewolf gene by learning too much about them. This book will teach you a lot about those hairy creatures of the night, so I want you to be extra careful while reading it.

If you notice any of the following things, STOP READING IMMEDIATELY:

- You find yourself looking at other humans and thinking *lunch.*
- You start to *notice smells* you never smelled before.
- You *growl at people* instead of talking to them.
- Your *nails begin to grow* at an alarming rate.
- You scratch your head in public *using your leg.*
- You greet your friends at the bus stop by *sniffing their butts.*
- You begin to grow hair in *all the wrong places.*

You've been warned.

Chapter One

Loser

Colin looked directly into the reflection staring back at him from the bathroom mirror and with absolute conviction said, "You are a loser."

His reflection agreed.

Much as he had done almost every day for the last year, Colin evaluated his body. He was tall for a thirteen year old, with lanky limbs and broad pointy shoulders that bordered on skeletal. His face looked to be at odds with the rest of his body with its gaunt features and perpetually dark circles beneath the eyes. Pale skin stood in stark opposition to his unruly dark and stringy hair. Trying to sharpen his vision, he squinted before fumbling with his glasses.

His reflection didn't look any better with them on.

After drying off, Colin got dressed and headed downstairs.

"Why are you dressed like that?" snapped his grandmother from her usual place in front of the TV. She hadn't even looked at him yet, not that it mattered. Colin didn't know what was more disturbing: that despite his grandmother being completely blind, she still watched TV religiously and commented on his clothes every day, or that he still felt the need to defend his choice of clothing to her. He was wearing jeans and an oversized hoodie.

"It's school today, Grandmother. I'm dressed for school," he murmured.

"I know that!" she spat.

Nothing wrong with her hearing, though.

"Do you need anything?" he asked.

His grandmother sipped tea from a china cup. "I can take care of myself, you little ingrate. Get to school. You're going to be late. If you don't get an education, I'll never get your lazy butt out of here."

There was no point in arguing.

"And comb your hair before leaving the house. I don't want people thinking I'm raising a hobo!" she said.

As Colin walked past the living room, his grandmother turned around in her chair and stared in his general direction with gray eyes damaged irreparably by cataracts. Blind eyes followed him as he walked to the door as quickly as he was able. It wasn't until he was outside with the door firmly closed behind him that he allowed himself to breathe again.

Colin's grandmother had always terrified him. He couldn't remember a time when she wasn't blind or cruel. Colin's parents lived in Seattle and over the past thirteen years had managed to have as little to do with their only son as humanly possible. They were young when his mother had discovered she was pregnant, and the following nine months had put a severe dent in their career plans. They were both up-and-coming lawyers at large firms, and as soon as they could be rid of Colin, they'd passed him off from one distant relative to another. Beyond that, they had no parental aspirations whatsoever.

Just over a year ago, after a short stint living with an uncle and aunt in Ohio, Colin had been sent to the small town of Elkwood to live with his only living close relative—his grandmother, Beatrice Strauss.

She hadn't welcomed him, there were no hugs, no loving relationship, just a bitter old woman who spent most of her days parked in front of the TV and commenting on what a disappointment Colin was. He'd tried to help her, but she never wanted it. Despite being blind, she was more than able to get around and take care of herself. The only time she left the house was to attend the monthly town hall meetings to which he was never invited.

Colin was twenty feet from the bus stop when the school bus flew by. The mocking grins of students plastered the bus's back window as it disappeared over the hill. Thankfully, the school was centrally located, which meant he'd be only slightly late.

On his way to school, Colin passed Mrs. Flipple, a kind old lady who walked her tiny, yappy dog, Jinx, each morning, rain or shine. As per usual, Jinx went straight for Colin, yapping in that high-pitched bark that only small, irritating dogs can make. Colin nodded politely to the old lady and held on to a secret hatred for that little dog.

The town was always overcast, and it rained almost every day of the year, which suited Colin's depressed personality. He was thankful he didn't live in a warmer climate as he'd have a much harder time being pale and awkward.

He'd survived the seventh grade at Elkwood School with above-average grades and a below-average number of friends. He was still considered a stranger here. His lack of personality, athleticism, and sense of humor didn't help in the slightest. He wasn't handsome enough to be popular or ugly enough to be ignored. He was just weird enough that students could be heard wondering aloud about him as he walked by. Now in the second week of his eighth grade year, Colin had one *sort of* friend, one unrealistic crush, and was the constant focus of several bullies who were determined to make his life miserable.

Loser.

He reached Elkwood School just as the second bell rang to indicate the start of classes. On average, each grade at the school contained only twenty to thirty students, and because of a limited number of teachers, some classes taught more than one grade or subject.

As Colin ran up the steps to the main entrance, a dark, looming shape confronted him. He looked up into the face of Principal Hebert.

"You're late again, Mr. Strauss." His voice sounded like rumbling thunder.

"I'm sorry, Mr. Hebert. I missed the bus."

"While I admire your use of a classical excuse, I'd

prefer if you'd made an attempt at originality. Had you been more creative, I would not feel the need to place you in detention."

"I'm really sor—"

"But as you're still trying to apologize rather than give me something interesting to work with, I'll be seeing you after school."

Colin studied his feet carefully. "Yes, sir."

"Run along." Mr. Hebert gestured, pushing his hand ahead of him in a forward motion.

Colin made his way into the building and chanced a glance back to see Principal Hebert slowly shaking his head. Hebert was a former marine and rumored war hero who had retired to Elkwood almost ten years ago and although he had absolutely no qualifications had been appointed as the school principal. He was a massive hulk of a man with the sort of physique that suggested he could bend large metal things with his bare hands. Principal Hebert was a firm believer in detention and hard work and often liked to combine the two. Most detentions involved cleaning something. Colin made a mental note that his day was not off to a rip-roaring start.

Can't get any worse.

Colin's day quickly got worse.

He moved down an empty corridor, his sneakers squeaking loudly on the clean laminate flooring before entering the last classroom on the right.

The entire class turned to look at him. Some groaned, others laughed, a few smirked. Mrs. Davenport was the substitute teacher again today for Biology, and she greeted him with a warm smile.

"Good morning, Colin. Please take a seat. We were just getting started."

Colin shuffled over to his seat next to Jeremy Rodson, the only person in Elkwood Colin could refer to as a friend. Everyone liked Jeremy even though he had never really joined one particular group. He played on the basketball team, so the jocks liked him. He was smart and maintained decent grades, so he was accepted by the smart kids. He was a good actor, so the creative types liked him. Colin had met him on his first day, and Jeremy had introduced him to the school. With so many commitments, Jeremy wasn't always around, so Colin was still forced to maintain his unhappy, loner lifestyle.

"No Mr. Winter again?" Colin asked quietly.

"Apparently he's sick," said Jeremy and grinned. "Why are you so late?"

"Missed the bus."

"Detention again?"

"Yup."

"Pay attention, boys," said Mrs. Davenport with a smile. She was flipping through a PowerPoint presentation about pheromones.

As the only substitute teacher in the small Elkwood School, Mrs. Davenport was never short of work. She was also the kindest teacher that Colin had ever encountered. Her presence had a calming effect on the students that Mr. Winter could never manage.

Mr. Winter was a jerk. It wasn't just Colin's opinion but more of a collective agreement throughout the entire school, including the teachers. An uptight individual in his late thirties, he had a particular hatred for students, teaching, other teachers, and did I mention, students? A few years ago, Mr. Winter's entire family—wife, parents, grandparents—had been killed in a car accident, and rumor had it that the insurance settlement had been sizeable. The rumor quickly proved true when Mr. Winter started travelling the better part of the school year.

"Pheromones indicate the availability of a female for breeding." Mrs. Davenport was met with a round of sniggers. "Well, it's true," she said calmly. "All animals excrete pheromones, and they can indicate a variety of things. Anything from sex to marking territory, and it can even act as a defense mechanism."

"Colin, you should get yourself some pheromones," said Gareth Dugan from behind a textbook. His cronies laughed in honor of their leader's display of wit.

Gareth was a bully with scraggly hair and a troubled complexion. Having been raised on a farm on the outskirts of Elkwood, Gareth had always struck Colin as being quite large for his age. Gareth didn't like Colin, but then, the feeling was mutual.

"Why would I need pheromones?" shot back Colin. "Your smell already overpowers everything in the room."

That probably wasn't smart.

The entire room agreed with him by sitting in absolute silence.

"That's enough," said Mrs. Davenport and cheerfully continued to describe other chemical factors that trigger social responses.

Colin dared a glance back to see Gareth glaring at him like a lion eyeing an injured antelope.

Gareth would inevitably seek revenge. Colin didn't

need a chemical factor to trigger a social response. All he had to do was open his mouth.

He tried his best to concentrate on his textbook, opened at random, but his thoughts remained fixed on how to save himself a beating Jeremy, who remained happily oblivious and completely free of any such dealings, leaned over enthusiastically.

"Did you take a look at Tori yet? Classic Tori outfit." He grinned and subtly tilted his head backward. Having developed earlier than any other girl in school, Tori was the blond bombshell of Elkwood. Okay, she was more like a small nuclear explosion. To aid the raging hormones of teenage boys, she made a habit of wearing low-cut shirts complimented by extremely short skirts.

Mrs. Davenport turned to the whiteboard, and Colin glanced back three rows on the right to see Tori conveniently perched on the edge of her stool wearing a short powder-blue skirt and knee-high boots.

Colin's eyes followed the curves of her body upward until he realized she was looking directly at him with a wry smile. He blushed instantly, but the awkward moment was suddenly interrupted as a textbook smashed into the side of his head, sending his glasses skittering across the desk and onto the floor.

The class laughed as Colin slipped from his stool and crawled around in front of the desk, searching for his glasses.

Mrs. Davenport whirled around, spied Colin on the floor, and asked, "What was that? Colin, what are you doing?"

"Sorry, Mrs. Davenport. Just looking for my glasses."

The bell rang before any further interrogation could

be made, and the class headed for the exit. Colin still couldn't find his glasses.

Ironic. If I was wearing my glasses, I'd have no trouble finding them.

The side of his head was throbbing from where the textbook had struck him. No doubt Gareth or one of his minions to thank for that.

Colin stood and came face-to-face with Becca Emerson, his heartbeat doubling in speed.

"I found your glasses," she said, handing them over.

"Uh, thanks, B-Becca."

The rest of the class had cleared out. He put on his glasses, and she came into focus. Around his height with fiery red hair and pale skin, Becca displayed a standoffishness that made most people avoid her. She wasn't developed like Tori, but neither were most cover models. Becca was a little like Jeremy in that she didn't associate with any one group, but where he belonged to everyone, she tended to avoid all people. Her dad was some sort of government worker, which translated to "spy" to most middle schoolers.

Becca always wore dark makeup and dark clothes making her look paler than she actually was. She maintained high grades, avoided large groups, and Colin had loved her since he first saw her. It was, of course, a secret love because there was no way he could ever work up the nerve to do anything about it.

"Are you okay?" she asked.

Oh, that voice.

"Uh, yeah. Just another head wound. Probably won't be the last." He attempted a half-hearted grin.

They awkwardly stared at each other as Colin's mind raced for something smart to say.

What do I say? You're gorgeous? Want to share a slushee? Marry me?

"Okay, well have a good day," said Becca, and left.

Smooth, Strauss. Very smooth.

Not the most suave guy at the best of times, Colin managed to be even less so around Becca. How would he ever be able to ask her out, let alone have an entire conversation with her if he didn't even manage to open his mouth?

***

Having made it to last period unscathed, Colin was busy staring at Becca as the minutes on the clock clicked by while he planned his escape. He would have to move fast, get out of the school, and off the grounds. He'd skip the bus altogether—

"Wonder what Hebert's going to have you do for detention today? My money is on cleaning the gym floor," said Jeremy.

Detention!

"I'm so screwed."

"It's not that bad, just cleaning."

"Not that," groaned Colin. "Gareth got detention in third period."

"Well at least you'll have company," said Jeremy unhelpfully.

The bell rang, and Colin's heart skipped a beat.

"Just once Jer, just once I'd love to be as oblivious as you are."

"You got detention today, Colin?" asked Becca.

Colin almost dropped his books. He hadn't noticed her approach. "Uh, yeah. I was late today."

"I know. I was there."

"Right."

"I was wondering if I could talk to you. Alone. I can walk you to your detention."

"I've got to run anyway. Catch ya later." And with that, Jeremy bounced off.

"Y-yeah, of course," said Colin. This was new territory. Other than the occasional passing pleasantry, Colin had never had a full conversation with Becca. They walked down the south corridor toward the detention room at the back of the school.

"I know it hasn't been easy for you," said Becca without looking at him. "It must be strange to move here. Most people are born here these days."

"Uh, yeah, I've heard that. No one ever moves to Elkwood."

"The people here aren't open-minded. They only know what they know. And who they know. This probably isn't making any sense."

"No. I mean, yeah. Well. No, no it's not."

Becca turned to him. Her eyes were a deep hazel color, he'd never noticed before. She put a hand on his shoulder, and suddenly his insides were on fire. It was only a moment, but Colin felt as if she was looking *through* him.

Colin was way beyond his comfort zone and didn't know what to do. Was he supposed to say something? Did she want him to kiss her? Or was he misunderstanding her? When it came to reading girls, he was dyslexic. On the flipside, Becca Emerson was actually touching him! With her actual hand! But then she took her hand away and for a moment looked sad.

"I'm sorry, Colin. I thought maybe ... but no." She sighed. "I don't know if you'll ever be able to see things clearly here."

Colin had no idea what she was talking about; he was still reeling from her touch and for once actually managed to say something. "Maybe you could help me?"

Did I just say that?

What was he thinking?

"I have to go. My dad will wonder where I am. Good luck in detention."

And just like that, she was gone.

The ominous voice of Principal Hebert floated down the hallway. "Nice of you to join us, Mr. Strauss. Are you going to just stand there, or do I need to drag you into detention?"

Colin entered the room, noting the other attendees. Two students, Micah and Nathaniel Cross, otherwise known as the goth twins. They were pale with black tattoos, long black coats, tight black clothing, and permanent frowns plastered across their faces. Gareth sat with his feet up, smirking at Colin.

"Listen up," began Principal Hebert. "You're here because you did something or you didn't do something. All I care about is what you do from here on out. Gareth and Colin, you're on garbage cleanup. Nathaniel and Micah, you'll be sweeping the gym floor. One hour, people, and then I expect you back for dismissal."

Colin's heart sank in his chest, down his legs, and through the floor. He was a dead man.

Gareth clapped his hands with false cheer. "All right, Colin, buddy. Let's get to it!"

They grabbed a couple of garbage bags and headed outside. Without saying a word, Gareth just started picking up garbage. Colin, braced for an attack and watched him for a moment before hesitantly bending to the task too. It was getting dark, and the rain made the job all the more miserable.

After half an hour, Gareth had vanished around the other side of the building, and Colin began to think that maybe he had been worrying needlessly.

As he rounded a corner toward the back of the school, he saw his mistake. Sam Bale and Kevin Hadfield were sitting on one of the permanent picnic benches. They both looked menacing, as usual. Backtracking quickly, Colin turned and bumped into Gareth who shoved him.

"Where you going, buddy?" He spat that last word.

Colin dropped his garbage bag and backed right into Sam and Kevin, who were standing behind him.

"We don't have to do this," pleaded Colin.

"You don't belong here, Colin," said Gareth.

"I know. You've told me before."

Gareth stabbed a finger to his chest. "And that smart mouth of yours really doesn't belong here."

"It's attached to the rest of my body; I really don't have a choice in the matter."

Gareth faked a punch, and Colin flinched.

"Please, just tell me what to do," begged Colin, fighting to keep the tears at bay. He'd been here before; he knew what was coming.

Kevin and Sam grabbed one of Colin's arms while Gareth stood inches from his face. His breath stank. "I want you to go away. That's all. You don't belong here. Sooner or later you'll get the message."

Gareth punched him hard twice in the stomach and then once in the kidneys. Colin dropped to the ground and curled into a ball. Sam and Kevin began kicking him and then stripped him down to his underwear until finally, they left. Colin lay sobbing on the cold ground, half-naked and in pain.

This had been Colin's life for over a year. Feeling like he'd failed at life in general, Colin had been reduced to living in a state of constant fear and humiliation. He had suffered bullying and his grandmother's hatred.

Colin knew he was a loser, but he hated that everyone else knew it too.

The only positive he could think of was Becca and the strange, brief conversation they had shared. He picked himself up, feeling his bruised ribs, wincing as he walked barefoot across the parking lot away from the school. Hebert would be angry that he didn't return for the end of detention, but he didn't care. He didn't intend to come back. He had to do something or he was going to end up dying here in Elkwood.

Colin decided he had to go to Seattle to see his parents Tonight.

Chapter Two

Unusual Meetings

Colin debated whether he should pack a toothbrush. Seattle was only a couple of hours north, and his parents would likely just stick him on a bus right back to Elkwood, so it was unlikely he'd need anything for an overnight stay.

Every time he'd been beaten up, Colin thought about going to see them. He even knew exactly how to do it.

He'd only met his grandfather once before he had passed away. The old man had been a mechanic and operated out of an old garage in Elkwood's rustic downtown. His grandmother had never seen fit to sell it so there it remained, gathering dust.

More important to Colin's plan, his grandfather's '83 Pontiac Phoenix, a boat of a car, still sat in the garage. Colin had learned to drive from one of his uncles during a six-month stint in Texas a few years ago. Uncle Cletus believed that every boy aged five and over should know how to drive, shoot, and skin things. Colin hadn't managed to master the skinning bit because the sight of blood made him dizzy. However, being fairly tall, he'd taken to driving quite easily.

He knew his grandmother kept the car's gas tank full and started it once a month although Colin had no idea why as she never drove it anywhere and, being completely blind, would likely run over several people and cause a fair amount of damage.

Colin planned to take the logging road in order to avoid the main highway for as long as possible. For a thirteen-year-old with no driver's license, no insurance, and driving a stolen car, getting pulled over in the middle of the night would be a bad situation.

"Just do it," said Colin to no one in particular.

He grabbed his jacket and backpack and headed out into the night. The rain had subsided, but the fog was lying low over the town, as it always seemed to on town hall meeting nights.

Colin took Twelfth Street out of the residential area and tried to look casual, which was pointless as no one was around.

The town hall clock began to chime nine o'clock. The meeting would be let out in another half an hour or so and with it, his grandmother. Best-case scenario, she would go home like normal, settle herself in front of the television and watch *Wheel of Fortune* re-runs, assuming he'd already gone to bed. The worst-case scenario would involve much more shouting and him being grounded for life.

The fog was getting thicker, turning the streetlights into growing balls of dull light. Colin could barely see twenty feet in front of him. Driving in this weather would be scary.

Suck it up, Colin; this has to be done.

Confidence wasn't Colin's strong point, but he was determined. With every step, his aching ribs reminded him just why he had to go through with this crazy idea.

He ducked into the alleyway behind Harrison's Grocers. One more block and he'd be able to go through the back door of his grandfather's garage using the keys he'd swiped from the kitchen drawer.

Colin was trying to remember all the important parts of getting a car going when he heard a set of footsteps. They were at the other end of the alleyway coming toward him. He really hadn't expected to encounter anyone. Elkwood was a sleepy town where people didn't stay out past 8:00 p.m., especially this late in the year. The only people out tonight should be those at the town hall.

Colin moved to the side of the alley and crouched down behind a dumpster, holding his breath for so long that he began to feel dizzy.

The footsteps were moving quickly.

"I hope you're sure about this," said a gruff voice. "Otherwise we just ended a town hall meeting early for no good reason. And you know how important they are."

Colin knew the voice; it was Becca's dad, Mr. Emerson. His rough tone was unmistakable even though Colin had only heard him speak a couple of times in passing when picking Becca up from school.

"It is for certain." The second voice came as a surprise

as Colin had only heard one set of footsteps. He didn't recognize this voice, but it was deep and hollow as if the man were speaking from the bottom of a well. It sent shivers throughout Colin's body, running from his toes to his spine, stopping at his head, and continuing back the way they came.

Mr. Emerson and his companion stopped walking. Colin could now see both strangers from his hiding place. Mr. Emerson had his back to him, but Colin could see that he was dressed in his usual dark suit. The man facing Mr. Emerson looked like he had stepped out of medieval times wearing a long, shabby cloak with the hood covering his head and face. Colin had certainly never seen him around town.

"What I want to know," said Mr. Emerson, "is why we didn't know about this sooner?"

"You know very well it's not as easy as that," said the cloaked figure.

Mr. Emerson stormed away down the alley. "I need to get up to the base. I assume you can find your way home." It was a statement, not a question, and then he was gone.

The cloaked stranger turned to walk away and then paused. Turning his hooded head as if looking for something in the dark alley, the stranger suddenly zeroed in on Colin's hiding spot. Colin held his breath. The stranger didn't move.

It seemed like an eternity although barely ten seconds had passed before the stranger turned away slowly and then spoke. "You should go now, Colin Strauss." The words hung in the air. "Or you will be late."

With that, the stranger glided down the alley without making a sound.

What in the world was that thing?

He emerged from his hiding place, carefully inspecting the alley. There was no sound, and the fog seemed to be lifting slightly. Whoever the creepy stranger was, he was right; Colin had to get moving. If the town hall meeting was already out, then that meant he was going to have a harder time getting out of town unseen.

He hurried the rest of the way, constantly checking behind him, afraid the cloaked stranger was following him and would emerge at any moment.

Or you will be late. Late for what?

Quietly slipping inside the garage, Colin finally allowed himself to breathe properly after locking the door behind him. His heart was racing, he was covered in sweat, and his nerves were on edge. He felt like he'd run a marathon.

If the town meeting had been broken up by some sort of urgent situation, then his grandmother would already be on her way home. He had to hurry.

The garage was exactly as it had been when his grandfather died and smelled like old cigarettes and motor oil.

Colin pulled open the wide double doors, checking the street to make sure it was empty. The fog was still heavy enough that he couldn't see past the end of the block.

The car started with a roar on the first turn. Tamping down his panic, he pulled the car out onto the street, parked, and quickly got out and closed the double doors.

Colin wasn't a lawbreaker, at least not normally. He was beginning to feel queasy. Maybe this was a mistake?

No, I'm committed. I have to do this.

They were his parents; at the very least, he had to let them know he was unhappy and being bullied incessantly. He had to do something!

He drove slowly down the street being careful not to give it too much gas. He'd almost made it the two blocks out of downtown when he hit the red light. There were only two stoplights in Elkwood, one by the school and this one that was activated by a crosswalk. He thought maybe it was a glitch as he couldn't see anyone, and then he saw her. His heart sank somewhere deep down into his stomach.

She walked out of the shadows of the old lawyer's office building and crossed the street. It was Becca Emerson!

What is she doing here?

She looked as pale as always, her red hair tied back, wearing her usual dark clothes.

Colin closed his eyes.

Please don't look. Don't look, don't look, just keep walking, don't look this way, just keep walking.

He opened his eyes. She was standing directly in front of his car wearing a stunned expression. Quickly regaining her composure, she walked around to the driver's window. Colin was no longer certain he was breathing. He inched the window down and gave his best effort at being calm.

"Oh, hi, Becca," squeaked Colin.

"Colin, what are you doing out here? You can't be out

here. The meeting ended early."

"Uhh, yeah I know. Grandmother just wanted me to start the old car and make sure the battery was okay," said Colin, drumming nervously on the steering wheel. Colin didn't lie well under normal circumstances, never mind while sitting in a stolen car about to take a road trip out of town in the middle of the night.

Becca eyed him suspiciously. "You have to get out of here now! No one's supposed to be out," she said, looking around as if expecting someone to step out of the fog at any time.

Something occurred to Colin. "What are you doing out here? Were you at the meeting?"

She looked taken aback. "No, well … no. Colin, you have to take this car back wherever you got it and get home. In fact, you should just drive straight home. Quickly."

Colin didn't know why Becca sounded so anxious, but he recognized an opportunity when he saw it. "You're probably right; I'll just drive home and bring the car back in the morning."

"Go, now!"

"Good night, Becca." But she was already walking away from the car and was quickly swallowed up by the fog.

Colin stepped on the gas and sped the rest of the way out of town. If he did pass anyone, he didn't realize it. He eased off the gas as he approached the old forestry road and wondered what could have got Becca so agitated? And why was she out so late anyway? Had she been at the town hall meeting?

Putting Becca out of his mind, he was determined to forget about his strange encounter with the cloaked stranger and Mr. Emerson, and concentrate on the task at hand.

Mustering up as much courage as he could, Colin turned onto the dark road, accelerating into the night.

Chapter Three

Dark Roads

Driving wasn't a difficult task; the car was old and bulky but so heavy that it hugged the corners. When he reached the one-mile marker out of town, the fog lifted, and it looked like the night would be clear from here on out.

Colin's mind blurred with thoughts of Becca, Mr. Emerson, his grandmother, his parents, the town meeting, his aching ribs, Gareth Dugan, the cloaked figure—it was all making his head hurt.

Concentrate on driving, Colin!

It wasn't long before the tall trees on either side of the road blocked his view, and he only occasionally caught glimpses of the bright, full moon. Colin had never travelled this road before and wasn't sure how far north it ran before joining the main highway.

The loud, cynical portion of Colin's brain continued

to argue that not only would his parents send him straight back to Elkwood, but they would probably dismiss his worry and misery as silly teenage stuff. At this depressing thought, Colin eased off the gas for a moment as he considered returning to Elkwood to face the wrath of his grandmother.

No, he was going. He stepped on the gas and flicked on the radio to take his mind off things.

Most of the stations Colin chanced upon contained the sweet rhythmic sounds of static, but occasionally, the old radio would grab a piece of a tune from an oldies station. As the road began its steep descent down to a tree-filled valley, an Elvis Presley song began to play, but then the song was gone again, replaced by a male voice shrouded in static.

"Alpha and beta units stay on him! If we lose him now, we may not get another chance," growled the voice.

Must be a radio play.

"He's too fast," responded a female voice. "What's the six on the chopper? We need it now! The trees are too dense, I repeat, the trees are too dense."

"Affirmative, beta unit. Chopper is en route," said the male voice.

Not a very interesting radio play.

But as there was nothing else on and at least the signal seemed to be clear, he just left the dial where it was.

"Alpha unit is down!" said a different male voice in a panic. "It just tore right through us. Jensen is down. Burke is missing! Oh God, this is a mess. Just a mess!"

"Pull yourself together!" ordered the first male voice. "You're a trained agent! Get it together! Where did the subject go?"

Agent? Subject? This is just lame.

"It's breaking east," said the second male voice. "No wait, south! It's heading south toward the logging road."

Logging road?

"This is Commander Emerson," interjected a familiar voice on the radio. "Don't let this thing get away, you hear me?"

"Mr. Emerson?" said Colin.

What am I listening to?

"Sir," came the female voice again, "we have a problem. There's a car coming down the logging road."

"What?" exclaimed Mr. Emerson. "How far?"

"It's on track to intercept with the subject. We're taking a shot at the subject, sir."

A gunshot ripped through the night air, and Colin took his foot off the accelerator, heart racing.

"We got him, sir!" said the female voice again. "He's injured! The subject is moving away from the road."

"And the car?" said Mr. Emerson.

"Still coming."

Colin didn't know what to do. Were they talking about his car? Was that really Mr. Emerson? What's the *subject*?

In a panic, he stepped on the gas, heart racing, hoping he'd be able to get out of the area entirely.

"Chopper support is inbound," said the original male voice.

"Commander Emerson! The subject ... we've lost him. No wait. He's cut back to the road!"

A massive creature burst out of the trees ahead of

Colin, stumbling across the road, illuminated by a blinding spotlight. The animal looked like an enormous wolf, bigger than any man, but it stood upright! Stopping in front of Colin's car, the creature turned its head and snarled.

Colin panicked and swung the car to the right, but the tires lost traction on the gravel and the old, heavy vehicle lurched headlong into the creature. The front window of the car smashed, and metal tore as the creature scraped its massive claws against the hood of the car. The tires finally caught some traction, sending the car arcing across and off the road where it crashed through the trees and down a steep embankment. The creature clung to the hood of the car and snarled ferociously.

Colin could hear deranged screaming and realized it was his own voice.

The old Pontiac hit something hard, and Colin smashed his head into the steering wheel as the car flipped forward, and then everything turned a murky black.

***

The world slowly spun back into focus and looked a lot like mud. Colin lay facedown on the ground, his heartbeat thundering in his ears. Or was it a helicopter? He remembered a helicopter. Mercifully, his glasses were still on his head but one lens was cracked.

Colin rolled over onto his back, and a searing pain shot through his left arm. He vomited, mostly on himself.

He pushed to his feet with his right hand but fell back to his knees, the ground unsteady beneath him, and he wanted more than anything to slip back into unconsciousness.

What had happened?

Moonlight shone through the trees and glanced off the chrome rims of his grandfather's car, which was upside down and on fire.

I crashed my grandfather's car.

With that particular realization, Colin thought of his grandmother's reaction and surged to his feet, stumbling toward the car.

I shouldn't be this close to a burning car.

He turned and staggered away, clutching his left arm close to his body.

How did this happen?

Colin could remember driving, he was listening to a radio show ...

He could hear a helicopter somewhere close, the low thump of the propellers resonating through the night air.

Then he'd hit something. No, something hit him?

Why can't I remember?

A low, guttural growl came from behind Colin, and everything flooded back to him.

The wolf! The massive wolf! Big teeth! Big, sharp-looking teeth. The kind that eat things. They were chasing it and then I hit it. My grandmother is going to be so upset.

Colin turned around slowly, watching as the area in front of the smashed car began to move. The moonlight was so bright here that even in his confused and injured state there was absolutely no mistaking what he was seeing.

The creature pulled itself up on all fours, its body covered with dark gray scraggly hair. But this was no wolf. Its body was more muscular, and it was the size of a small horse. Colin watched in stark horror as the creature put an enormous hairy hand on the Pontiac and pushed itself to its feet. It had a hand, not a paw! And feet! It reached its other hand up and rubbed its head. It growled again.

The creature's large ears twitched as Colin took a step back. Time slowed down as the creature whipped around its head and in two long strides was looming over him.

Colin cowered. He wasn't sure if he was actually cowering—he'd never done it before, he might be doing it wrong. He was shaking and sweating all over. The creature bent over and lowered its head level with Colin's. It was definitely some sort of a wolf. It had a wolf's head. A snout protruded from the center of its face and began sniffing him with huge nostrils as two dark golden eyes studied Colin intently.

What were you supposed to do when confronted with a wild animal? All he could think of was to assume the fetal position, but he thought that was mainly for bears. The creature's head whipped around as they heard a crash off to the right followed by the sound of an engine roaring. With the creature's attention focused elsewhere, Colin noticed that the animal was bleeding. Its chest and stomach area weren't as thickly covered in hair, and there was a bullet wound through its abdomen. Blood was matting the fur together.

"You've been shot," said Colin.

The creature turned back to Colin and looked down at the wound.

Something crashed again as Colin realized that the helicopter sounded like it was getting closer.

Looking like it was trying to decide what to do, the creature finally dropped down to all fours and fixed its golden eyes on Colin who had backed up against a tree.

The animal closed its eyes and lowered its head. It looked tired, and Colin thought he heard it sigh. Time slowed again as the creature sprang forward pinning Colin against the tree with those dangerously sharp-looking clawed hands. Colin screamed in pain as the animal grabbed his left arm, opened its jaws, and sank its teeth deep into Colin's forearm. The pain he'd originally felt from his injured arm was nothing compared to what followed.

Heat rushed through Colin's body; it felt like fire was consuming him from the inside out. His bones felt too big for his body, and his heart was hammering against his chest. The creature released his arm, turned, and fled into the night as a truck crashed through the trees in pursuit. They never noticed Colin leaning against the tree doing his best attempt to not die.

What was happening?

Colin retched again, trying to vomit, but nothing came out. He doubled over in pain, his body convulsing as spasms wracked him so violently he thought his spine would snap.

I'm dying!

Suddenly, the world in front of him exploded in vivid colors; he could smell the mustiness of his grandmother's old car mixed with the smell of leaking fuel and the flames. As the helicopter flew overhead once again, Colin heard a howl, and for a brief, insane moment, he thought he should answer. Colin's skin began to feel tight, and his brain felt like it was splitting apart in his skull. Without warning, his grandmother's car exploded, throwing flames toward the shining full moon as the world faded into a bright white nothingness.

Chapter Four

Dreams and Delusions

Colin was running. Well, he might have been Colin, he wasn't sure anymore. He ran low to the ground, moving much faster than Colin had ever moved in his life. Dry leaves crunched under his feet and foliage whipped against him as he ran. It felt so good to just run. Running was so freeing. An exhilaration that burned through his veins like iced water.

The darkness didn't hinder him in the slightest. Colin was aware of everything around him. He knew he was heading up hill; he could hear water in the distance, a stream maybe. He could smell animals in the forest, each one giving off its own individual signature, and he felt hunger. Hunger like he had never experienced before. It wasn't just the need for nourishment; it was the need to hunt. To feel warm flesh and bone crunch in between his teeth, to—

What's wrong with me?

Colin realized he was standing on a rainy street in a gloomy part of a city. He was watching and waiting. A dirty looking man in raggedy clothing left a store with bars on the windows and glanced up and down the street. Colin looked down at his hands and realized they weren't his own. He was seeing through someone else's eyes.

The dirty man made his way to a beat-up car, and Colin could literally smell him from across the street. Through the fresh rain, through the putrid stench of exhaust from the city itself, he could smell the filth on the man. The blood. The dirt under his fingernails. It made his stomach turn. And then Colin moved. It seemed like such a small motion, but one moment he was standing still, and a moment later he was next to the dirty man who turned and looked at him. Panic spread across that grimy face.

"No! Not you! Please—"

He was running again. Through the night, across a field. The night was overcast, and fog floated low, creating an ominous ceiling effect, but it didn't matter. He felt the moon up there somewhere, and it felt comfortable. Like a mother watching over a baby.

And then he was in an apartment. The furniture didn't match, and the walls were stained yellow from smoke. It had to be smoke; the apartment reeked of it. A mirror hung crooked on the wall, and the reflection Colin saw looking back at him was not his own. This new, not-Colin's jaw was angular, and he looked like he hadn't shaved in days. His hair was tousled, and his eyes ... there was something haunting about his eyes.

A woman in an ill-fitting bathrobe and badly colored hair screamed at Colin. "Don't you take him! He's a good boy. He is a good boy."

Colin's voice was deep and raspy. "He's a murderer. I'm sorry. I don't want to do this."

"Then leave. I'll take care of him. I'll keep him out of trouble."

"I'm sorry. It has to be this way."

Colin pushed his way past the woman who fell sobbing to the floor. Opening a door adjoining the living room, he found a boy, maybe eighteen or nineteen, huddled naked on the bed. Covered with dirt, his hair was matted to his head, the boy didn't even look at Colin; he just stared at one of the walls.

"You're him, aren't you? The one they talk about?" the boy whispered.

Colin didn't say anything; he reached for the boy and—

—was back in the field, only this time he was close to a farmhouse. It was a large house, and Colin felt like he recognized it. Leaping the low wall that ran around the property, Colin paced back and forth across the garden.

This is Becca Emerson's house.

The information came to him distinctly. He could smell her. She was up there in one of the rooms. That fresh soapy smell mixed with the odd perfume she wore that smelled like Twizzlers. And he could hear her breathing, she was asleep. Her heartbeat was steady. *Thump. Thump. Th—*

Colin was lying in bed. A big bed in a dark paneled wood room lit with candles. Two older women and a man with a stone-faced scowl stared down at him. They were dressed strangely, as if they were from the past. This was a different time completely. He raised a hand and looked at it. It was pale and dainty. He had a woman's hand! He looked down at himself. He had women's breasts too! The scowling man made a grunting sound.

"I've never seen anything like it," he said. "She's feverish, but the injury she sustained last night is gone, like it never was."

"What do you mean?" Colin asked in a voice that was definitely not his own.

"Don't panic, dear. Try not to move. You're ill," said one of the ladies.

"What happened to me?"

"You were attacked," said the man. "Some sort of beast. A monstrous thing if I ever—"

Colin was standing at the end of a long dirt road next to a battered old mailbox. At the end of the driveway, he could see a shack of a house. He was surrounded by fields of corn and beyond them, vast rocky mountains. He looked down at his hands. They were large and worn. Farmer's hands.

An old man rode up on a horse and reined it to a stop. "Fletcher," said the old man. "It's happened again!"

"Not another one," replied Colin in a deep baritone.

"The same as before. It's impossible. Tore the thing to pieces."

"It makes no sense. Nothing could do that." But Colin didn't really believe that, or maybe the man whose eyes he was seeing didn't believe it. He felt nervous.

"That's the fourth cow this month. I've never seen

anything like this. The claw marks are … they're not natural!"

"I'll keep watch tonight."

The old man pulled on the reins and turned the horse around. "You kept watch last night and a whole lot of good that did us!" The old man spurred the horse into a gallop and raced off down the dirt driveway toward the house.

Colin felt relief and then guilt and then—

He nestled quietly in the undergrowth. He couldn't remember why he was doing this. He knew his name was Colin. He remembered Becca. He remembered school. He remembered … nothing else really. Just shadows. He remembered the deer because it chose that moment to step into view. Colin crept lower. The deer was at least twenty feet away, and it'd be hard to cover the distance, but Colin was hungry, so very hungry. The deer's heartbeat was racing; it knew something wasn't right. It would bolt! Colin leaped at the deer clearing the twenty feet as if it was a single step. He plowed into the startled creature and clamped his enormous jaws around the deer's throat and rippe—

He was caged. He growled and snarled and clawed with massive, hairy hands at the bars. It was dark and stormy, and he was out in the open, surrounded by rocks. He threw himself at the cage bars, but the metal was too thick. Chanting was coming from men wearing hooded robes who surrounded the stone circle, swaying back and forth to their song. Colin wanted to tear them to pieces. *No!*

This wasn't him. He wasn't this caged thing. He grabbed one of the bars with both hands and pulled with all his strength, and the bar gave way. The chanting stopped as he grabbed another bar and ripped it from its holding. And then another, and another, until Colin squeezed through the bars to feel the heavy rain dampening his fur as he stretched to his full height; he must be over seven feet tall! Colin could see the men running away through the dark night, and he could smell their fear. He liked a good run. Dropping to all fours, he raced off in pursuit, kicking up dirt as he—

He lay chained to a table in a white laboratory surrounded by men in white coats and surgical masks observing him. Colin began to panic as he tried to move his arms but they were restrained to the table.

"What are you doing to me?" said Colin in a young sounding voice.

"It's quite all right, son," answered one of the doctors. "We just want to examine you and study that thing inside you."

"What thing? What are you talking about? Where's my dad? What happened at the cabin?"

A nurse appeared with a syringe.

"What are you going to do with that?" asked the boy.

"Just relax," said the nurse.

Colin felt a pin prick, and then the world turned woozy and—

He was in what looked like a cave, or maybe a catacomb, flickering torches hanging from the walls, the air was musty and old. Looking down at the body he now inhabited, Colin noted he was naked and, thankfully, a man. His left foot was shackled to the wall by a long, rusty chain.

Thirteen men in white hooded robes that hid their faces stood in front of him. One swung incense while another read from a book. It sounded Italian or maybe Spanish. Colin had never been any good with languages. But he could smell the fear in the men or priests or whatever they were. And it made him angry. "Let me go!" said Colin. His voice was low and guttural. Commanding.

The priests didn't move, and the reader continued.

"If you don't let me go, you're all going to be sorry," said Colin.

The reader pulled back his hood to reveal a cross tattooed on his forehead. The old man was bald, and his skin had a weathered quality that looked like he'd spent time at sea. He smelled of incense and fear.

"It is not right that you exist, my son," said the priest, making the sign of the cross. "You are not fit for this world. Whatever manner of evil brought this upon you, we will extinguish it here tonight."

"You're an idiot," said Colin. "I feel amazing. There is nothing wrong with me."

"You have killed without remorse," accused the priest.

"I killed thieves and murderers. I did a service. This power I have, it's good."

"You are possessed, my son."

"And who are you that you think you can take it away from me?"

"We are the ones that would protect you."

"I will tell you one last time. Let me go."

"This we cannot do," said the priest.

"So. Be. It."

Colin felt something inside him surge. Like

butterflies in your stomach at first, then quickly turning into a burning sensation that raced through every limb, muscle, and sinew. The hair on his arms stood on end, and bone began to crack as Colin screamed. The priests ran in a panic, trying to escape the catacomb as Colin was consumed in blinding pain—

Colin sat up in bed in a cold sweat. It was his own bed. He wasn't a man, a woman, large dog, or anything else unnatural. He was just Colin. And he was in his bed. The illuminated numbers on his alarm clock read 6:00 a.m.

How did I get home? Did I dream everything?

He tried to piece together the events from the night before. He remembered sneaking out while the town meeting was on and stealing his grandfather's car to go see his parents. He remembered the alley and Mr. Emerson and the strange man. He remembered driving out of town and seeing Becca, and he remembered turning onto the forestry road ... but nothing else. Horrible dreams had plagued his sleep. Something to do with blood and priests and ...

It was like trying to pick up water with a pair of tweezers. He couldn't fully remember anything.

Chapter Five

Got Change?

Sneaking across the hall so as not to disturb his grandmother, Colin crept into the bathroom, carefully closing the door and locking it. After unsuccessfully trying to recall the events of the previous night, Colin decided a shower was the best course of action. He felt grubby, for lack of a better word. He looked at his reflection in the bathroom mirror. Still the same loser as yesterday and the day before and the day before that. His reflection looked back at him, still in agreement.

Colin removed his underwear, which apparently was the only thing he had slept in, and turned on the hot water. Stepping into the shower and closing his eyes, Colin let the water pour over his face and body. He fumbled for the soap on its usual ledge and turning around, opened his eyes, coming face to face with a giant wolf-man. It was standing in his shower looking down at him. Colin didn't scream or shriek; he just slipped easily into a blind panic, dropping the soap, and tried to scramble out of the shower, slipped on the soap he had dropped, and fell backward toward the creature. He made a grab for the shower curtain, missed, and collapsed into the bathtub again. He'd expected to fall into the creature, but it was gone as if it had never been there in the first place. Colin scrambled up, flinging the curtain open to see if the creature was in the bathroom.

It wasn't.

But his grandmother was.

She stood in the open doorway, ninety pounds of bitter old woman with bright pink rollers in her hair and wearing an ancient looking nightgown. Her blind eyes stared in Colin's direction who unnecessarily covered his private areas with his hands, looking sheepish.

"Uh, Grandma, I ... "

"You're making a lot of noise!" barked his grandmother.

"I'm sorry. It was just—"

"How am I supposed to get my beauty sleep with you in here treating my bathtub like it's a playground?"

"I ... I slipped."

"Frightened me half to death banging around like that!" His grandmother stepped out and slammed the door. "And lock the door when you use the bathroom!" she called from behind the door.

I did lock the door. Didn't I?

Colin tried to recall, but his memory was playing tricks on him. He closed the curtain and quickly washed. Shutting off the water, he opened the curtain and then closed it again. Something had caught his eye. There was a rip in the shower curtain, four rips to be exact. Four perfect gashes that sliced diagonally across the curtain.

Creepy.

Colin's brain was a logical one, not really all that creative unless you count some marginally impressive finger paintings he'd done in the third grade. The sketchy memory from the previous night, the giant creature he hallucinated in his shower, the gash in the shower curtain, the locked bathroom door. None of it made any sense, and that troubled Colin. It troubled him while he dried off, it troubled him when he got dressed, and it troubled him as he walked down the stairs.

His grandmother had already taken her place in front of the TV, so Colin ducked into the small kitchen and made himself a bowl of cereal. Still hungry, he ate two cartons of yogurt and drank the remainder of the milk. After the milk, he made some toast and piled it with peanut butter.

I'm so hungry! What is wrong with me?

Once he had consumed the toast, he started searching the pantry and for the lack of anything better, ended up eating an entire package of beef jerky. He was happily tearing through the dried meat when he was suddenly very aware of the time.

School!

Colin raced down the hallway and out the front door before his grandmother had a chance to bark at him for being late/dressing strange/being an idiot. The sky was overcast as usual, and parts of Elkwood were shrouded in fog. Colin ran for the bus stop but arrived just in time to see the retreating taillights of the school bus. Another day of being late. Maybe even another detention.

Great. No memory, hallucinations, and the appetite of a bear after hibernation. How can this day get any worse?

And then it started raining.

***

Colin arrived onto school grounds as the bell rang to indicate the beginning of class, his heart sank as he rounded the corner of the main building and came face to face with Principal Hebert.

"Well hello, Mr. Strauss. First you skip out on checking in after detention yesterday and now you're late once again. I have the distinct feeling of deja vu. Might you be sharing the same feeling this morning?" said Principal Hebert.

"I'm sorry, Mr. Hebert. I—"

"Miss the bus again, did we?"

"Well, yes, but well, you see—"

"Oh, there's more?" said Principal Hebert. "Come on, Mr. Strauss. Enlighten me."

Colin stared at Principal Hebert. Principal Hebert stared back. People were always trying to push Colin into doing things he didn't want to. He hated that feeling. Maybe it was the disorientation, the food, maybe even the weather was finally getting to him but he decided to do something about it.

"Last night I tried to run away, met a floating man in a back alley, and then blacked out and ended up back in my bed. This morning when I woke up, I found a giant wolf-man in my shower and then I ate half the contents of my kitchen. And that, Mr. Hebert, is why I'm late."

Colin's chest hurt, his pulse was racing, and he felt like he was going to have a heart attack.

Principal Hebert raised an eyebrow. "That's much more interesting than you missing the bus, Mr. Strauss. Try and make it on time in future."

Colin slowly sidestepped around the large, scary authoritarian and ran up the rest of the steps into the building.

Once inside, he leaned against a wall. His heart was trying to pound out of his chest, and he had a splitting headache. At a water fountain, Colin threw some water on his face, trying to collect himself.

He knocked lightly on the door to the biology classroom and pushed open the door.

"Mr. Strauss!" barked Mr. Winter.

Colin actually jumped. He'd been expecting Mrs. Davenport again, but it looked like Mr. Winter was feeling better.

"Take a seat quickly please. We have a lot to cover, and I'm in no mood for your tardiness today."

Colin slouched his way to the empty stool next to Jeremy who was looking his usual spritely self.

Leaning over, Jeremy asked in a whisper, "Detention again?"

Colin shook his head. "Let me off with a warning."

"Today we're going to study the brain," said Mr. Winter. "Although most of you seem to be missing yours, there's no reason not to study it in case you happen to come across one. While I fully expect the majority of you to fail the inevitable test that will follow our line of study today, I do encourage you all to try your hardest despite the fact you're all idiots."

This was new. Mr. Winter was cruel and callous often alluding to insults and playing on the edge of being rude. But this was much too straightforward, even for him.

Maybe he's still not feeling well.

"Turn to page thirty-four in your textbooks and start reading." Mr. Winter sat down at his desk and closed his eyes.

Colin looked to Jeremy for an answer, but his friend just shrugged.

The rest of the class started reaching for their textbooks, so Colin did the same. His head felt like it was trying to split in half. It felt like his brain was humming, a sort of buzzing or static sound.

"You okay, Colin?" said Jeremy. "You look a little pale."

The entire class was beginning to notice him.

Colin stared at Jeremy who was still talking, but Colin couldn't hear him over the static in his head. He looked back at the rest of the class. All the usual suspects were present. Tori was seductively tracing her pen along her jaw line while she read.

That buzzing!

Gareth Dugan was in his usual spot along with Kevin Hadfield, but henchman number two, Sam Bale, was absent today.

There was Becca, looking gorgeous like always. Her eyeliner was especially dark today. Either that or she was just really tired.

The goth twins, Micah and Nathaniel, were sitting together in the back, staring at Colin. That was weird in itself, but what really tipped the scales was that they both looked incredibly worried. Or angry. He couldn't tell.

Colin lurched unnaturally as he lost control of his body and almost fell off his stool. Jeremy was shaking him. The buzzing in his head was numbing, he could barely hear anything, and the splitting pain in his head almost blinded him. He wiped a hand across his face and it came away wet. He was sweating. Not just sweating, he was practically leaking.

Finally, a bit of popularity.

Colin smiled drunkenly and fell off his stool but quickly scrambled to his feet.

"What on earth is going on, Mr. Strauss?" snapped Mr. Winter.

Colin staggered toward the door using the tables as support and muttered something about the bathroom. He crashed out of the door and collapsed in the hallway as Mr. Winter started to shout something but was cut off as the door swung shut.

The floor felt cool on his face, but he scrambled to his feet and made his way down the hallway toward the bathroom. He couldn't seem to get his arms and legs to work properly.

Managing to turn on a tap, he splashed water on his already damp face.

As he looked up into the mirror, Colin was astonished to see the wolf creature from his morning shower standing right behind him, snarling. Colin spun around to face an empty bathroom, and he started to laugh. It sounded somewhat maniacal; the sort of laughter you might hear in a mental institution. Unexpectedly, the buzzing stopped, the blinding pain subsided, and he regained full control of his gangly limbs once again.

He looked at his reflection. Same Colin. He was double-checking the bathroom to make sure there was no large, hairy, scary-looking creature lurking in any of the stalls when Jeremy burst in. "Jeremy! You scared me!"

"Are you okay? Winter sent me to check on you, but you look more like yourself now. What happened back there? And was that you laughing before I came in here?"

Colin shrugged. "I don't know. I really don't know. I couldn't hear. There was this buzzing sound. I think I might be going crazy, Jer."

"You were growling in class."

"Growling?"

"Yeah, like a dog. Did you get contacts?" said Jeremy.

"What? No, I ..."

Colin felt his face for his glasses.

I forgot my glasses?

"I thought you were blind without those things?"

"I ... geez, Jer. I have no idea what's going on with me. There was this whole thing last night with a car and then Becca was there, and I keep seeing this—"

"What? What are you seeing?" suddenly Jeremy got excited. "Are you hallucinating? Because that would be awesome."

Colin just looked at Jeremy, but despite the joke, he could see his friend's worry. "I'm sure it's nothing."

"You sure? Do you want me to take you to the nurse?"

"No, I'm feeling much better." Colin hurriedly assured his friend. "Maybe I'm getting the flu or something." The Elkwood School nurse was a monster of a woman called Mrs. Turnbull who had never heard the term *bedside manner*. She also didn't like to be interrupted, ever. Only the truly sick students of Elkwood ever went to Mrs. Turnbull's office.

"And the glasses?"

"I've been eating a lot of vitamin A lately?"

Jeremy gave him one of those slow blinking low stares that clearly said *you're kidding, right?*

Mr. Winter burst into the bathroom, slamming the door hard against the wall. "Back to class, Mr. Rodson!"

"Yes, sir," said Jeremy, making a quick exit.

Mr. Winter waited until the door was closed and then grabbed Colin by the shirtfront, pushing him hard up against the wall. "Just what do you think you're doing disrupting my class? Do you know how important biology is? It's everywhere! It's in me, it's in you, it's all over the place, and no one really understands it, so that's why we have to study it! Do you understand me, boy?"

Colin was too shocked to speak. A teacher was attacking him! Mr. Winter's eyes looked different. Like he was on drugs or something. The muscles in his face were tense and strained.

Colin nodded.

"Now get your ugly, useless, self back to class and read the chapter! Idiot!" Mr. Winter released Colin and stormed out of the bathroom muttering. "They're all idiots, ignorant idiots, all of them."

This day cannot get any worse. Or weirder.

***

After lunch and third period French, Colin's day did somehow manage to get much worse and a lot weirder. Jeremy had opted for Spanish as his foreign language, so Colin normally sat alone in French class. For today, Madame Frontier suggested they take part in group conversations, quickly splitting the class into three small groups of five students each. Colin got stuck with Kevin Hadfield, who was more interested in doodling in his biology textbook. The goth twins and Becca were also in his group, which was the only bright shining point in an otherwise scary and crappy day.

"Colin, are you feeling okay? You didn't look well earlier," asked Becca, sounding concerned.

"He always looks like that," said Kevin. "It's called ugly, and it's not curable."

Nathan and Micah simply stared at Colin.

"Yeah, I feel better. Just a dizzy spell."

"Why don't you have your glasses today?" said Becca.

Why does everyone notice that today? Yesterday I could have come to school naked and painted purple, and no one would have noticed a thing.

"I got contacts," said Colin quickly.

"You have nice eyes."

"You have nice eyes," mimicked Kevin in a whiny voice.

Micah and Nathan still hadn't blinked.

"Are you guys okay?" inquired Colin to the twins. They continued staring.

"Everyone should be speaking French. Remember your pronunciations," trilled Madame Frontier.

"They must like your eyes too, Colin," sneered Kevin. "How are those ribs today. Heard you took a nasty tumble during detention?"

"No, they're good. You must have heard wrong. Or maybe you're just such a moron that you have no concept of reality," Colin shot back. "Maybe your chronic stupidity is getting the better of you and soon you'll take that final step to becoming nothing more than a drooling vegetable."

What am I doing?

Becca stared open-mouthed. The twins looked ill. Kevin didn't know what to say; he just stared.

"Uh, sorry," said Colin. "I don't know what came ... uh ... over me."

"No, come on, Colin. Tell me more," spat Kevin. "You were up to the part where I'm a drooling vegetable."

The headache was back again. Colin's vision began to swim, and he put his head down and rubbed his temples.

What is wrong with me?

He wanted to lash out, tell Kevin exactly what he thought about him.

You're an idiot, a lackey, a lowlife coward who hides behind Gareth Dugan because you don't know how to look after yourself. You're a follower, a sheep, and not a smart sheep, the dumbest possible sheep you could ever imagine. And you smell. You smell like old farts and engine oil. That's what I think of you.

That's what he wanted to say but of course he would

never say that out loud.

"So I'm a dumb, stinking sheep, am I?" said Kevin.

"Wait, what?" said Colin.

"I'm sure he didn't mean that, Kevin," Becca hastily reassured him. "Tell Kevin you didn't mean that, Colin."

I didn't say that out loud, did I?

"I'm going to tear you apart, Strauss. As soon—"

"Wait, you heard me? Just now? But I didn't say—"

Oh, Colin. Why are you doing this? It was Becca's voice, but her lips hadn't moved.

The smell. Can't take the smell. It's getting worse. Micah's voice!

Colin looked around the class as fire burned through his brain. He could hear everyone, not just their voices, but their thoughts! All jumbled together in a horrible mess. Talking about food, French class, dating, clothing, TV shows, next period, last period, goats, Tori's latest outfit, where was Sam Bale, did Colin get beaten up last night, how tired they were, while others daydreamed. A maelstrom was spinning in his brain, and then as quickly as it arrived, it was gone.

"I'm not even going to wait until after class. I'm going to kick the crap out of you right here!" Kevin lunged at Colin but missed by a mile, collapsing into the now empty chair and onto the floor in front of the twins. Colin was now standing three feet away behind Becca's chair. Madam Frontier shouted in French.

"What the … ?" said Kevin.

And then the twins both vomited in unison. All over Kevin.

Becca grabbed Colin's shirt and dragged him out of

the classroom, away from the shrieks of Kevin Hadfield and what appeared to be the never-ending stomach contents of the goth twins. Madam Frontier fluttered around the classroom trying to regain order.

Becca didn't stop walking until they were outside the building, not far from where Gareth, Sam, and Kevin had jumped Colin the evening before.

An exhausted Colin slumped down onto a picnic bench while Becca stared hard at him.

"Why do people keep staring at me today?" mumbled Colin helplessly.

"Well, after you fell out of biology class this morning and whatever the hell just happened now, do you really have to ask? What's going on, Colin?"

"I honestly have no idea. I keep getting this headache. And I feel dizzy. Must be the flu. Maybe I'm getting whatever the twins have?"

"Where were you going last night when I saw you in town?"

"Are you writing a book or something?" snapped Colin. *What is wrong with me? I don't talk like this?*

"Don't be that way. I'm just trying to put the pieces together. You're not yourself at all."

Colin looked up at Becca. She looked genuinely concerned. Through the dark makeup, he could see her blue eyes shining down at him.

You're beautiful, like an angel.

"Look, I appreciate a good compliment, but that's just corny." Becca smiled. "And what are you? A ventriloquist now, I didn't even see your lips move."

"You heard me say that? Out loud?"

"Is this what puberty is like for a guy? And I thought girls had it bad."

They both laughed. The school PA system crackled to life, and Principal Hebert's voice boomed over the loud speaker.

"I need everyone's attention. I just received some distressing news. I would prefer that everyone to hear it from the sheriff's department but no one is available right now and it's better you hear it here first rather than second- or third-hand elsewhere."

There was a distinct pause. Colin looking out across the football field and through the fog could just make out a figure on the other side of the field. It looked like a man, wrapped in a long jacket, his face covered by a hood. Colin's stomach lurched as he realized the figure was watching him. Even more disturbing, Colin could smell the man, and the scent was familiar.

"The body of one of our grade eleven students, Samuel Bale, has been found at the northern edge of Merton Forest," continued Principal Hebert. "His parents didn't realize he was gone until this morning, and one of the Merton's farmhands found the body early this morning. The Elkwood Sheriff's Department is on site now. To dispel any rumors or gossip, he appears to have been attacked by an animal. This is a tragic day for Elkwood, and our thoughts and prayers go out to the Bale family. Under the circumstances, we will be dismissing everyone early today for the weekend. A funeral and burial will be held Sunday, and a grief counselor will be available here at the school on Monday if anyone needs to talk to someone."

The PA screeched as the ancient system shut off.

Becca said something hurriedly and ran back into the school. Colin didn't hear her anyway. The only thing that rang inside his head were the words *attacked by an animal.*

Coldness seeped into Colin's bones as shards of memory pricked along the edges of his brain. He couldn't fully grasp why, but something didn't feel right.

He looked back across the football field, but the stranger in the fog was no longer there.

Chapter Six

An Unexpected Visit

An eerie quiet had settled over the school as the students slowly left the grounds. Despite Principal Hebert's direct delivering of the news, it came as a shock to absolutely no one that the entire student body was developing their own theories on what actually happened.

Colin had returned to French class to retrieve his backpack, but everyone had already left. All that remained was a disturbing amount of vomit, and Colin couldn't help but feel a small stab of sympathy for Eric the janitor who would have to figure out how to get the stain out of the carpet. The goth twins were seldom apart and did most things together, but throwing up in unison? That was taking the *twins* thing a bit far.

Exiting the main building along with the last few stragglers, he was just in time to see Becca duck into the backseat of her father's black sedan. Mr. Emerson looked unhappy and as imposing as ever. As the car pulled away, Becca looked back at Colin, and his heart skipped several beats. At least *that* was a normal reaction.

Near the main gate, Colin could see some tenth graders making fun of Kevin Hadfield who was still mostly covered in puke but didn't seem to notice anything. One of his friends had just been killed.

Puked on and then one of his only friends gets mauled by a wild animal.

Colin wished he could feel sorry for Kevin but remembering what he had put him through for the past year made it next to impossible.

As Colin walked down across the school grounds, he picked up bits and pieces of gossip from huddled groups of students.

"—heard Sam and Gareth got into a fight last night and Gareth threatened to beat him to death!"

"—no wild animals in Elkwood that could do that."

"—demon hamster. I bet that's what it was."

"Did you hear the goth twins projectile vomited in Fren—"

"—so sad. I always thought Sam was cute."

"—brother heard from his cousin who works with the coroner. There were bits of Sam all over the—"

"—had to be Gareth Dugan."

Gareth was a bully, degenerate, and evil incarnate, but he was definitely not a wild animal. In no hurry to see his grandmother, Colin decided to walk home. He had a lot to think about.

Were people hearing his thoughts or was he hearing theirs? What's with the headaches? The puking? The stranger on the football field? His blackout? Thinking about it all together proved to be depressing.

Colin decided to get at least one of his questions answered by stopping by his grandfather's old garage. He smeared the grime across the front window with the sleeve of his sweater and peered through the clean spot. The car was definitely gone. Nothing but an empty space remained where the old car had been resting peacefully until Colin had liberated it last night.

Where did I leave the car?

The garage flashed before him, and he once again saw smoke and a helicopter, a large creature, like the one in his shower, searing pain, a howl, running through the woods ... a cascade of images that caused Colin to stagger backward off the sidewalk and into the road.

Even though the vehicle screeched to a halt, Colin still took most of the impact.

Upon collision, his visions disappeared, and he simply lay in a crumpled heap in the middle of the road.

"Colin! Holy crap, Colin! Are you okay?" Jeremy's voice.

"You hit me with your car."

Jeremy was crouching next to him. "Well, my mom technically hit you. You came out of nowhere; we couldn't have missed you if we'd tried."

"You could have at least tried," protested Colin, rolling onto his back. The initial pain was horrific, but now he actually didn't feel that bad.

"Hi, Colin, you okay?" called Jeremy's mom, cheerily leaning out her window. Mrs. Rodson shared her son's ignorance for normal things, like hitting someone with your car for example. Nothing ever seemed to bother the Rodsons. It was a bit weird, but they seemed to fit into Elkwood quite well.

"You dented the fender," Jeremy pointed out unhelpfully.

"I'm fine, thanks, Mrs. Rodson. And I'm sorry, Jer. I didn't mean for my body to damage your car."

"Well, I guess it's okay. Dad can probably just hammer it back out."

That was Jeremy. Completely immune to sarcasm. Some days Colin believed that Jeremy was barely human. He was just too oblivious to everything.

"Should I call 9-1-1?" said Jeremy.

"No, I think I'm actually okay." Colin sat up and then got to his feet.

"Wow, you can really take a hit. I thought for sure you'd broken something, maybe some internal bleeding."

"Your optimism is really what keeps me going."

"Hey, what are friends for?"

Oblivious.

"Hey, can you give me a ride home?" said Colin.

"Of course we can, dear," said Mrs. Rodson. "It's the least we can do."

Before, Colin had been in no hurry to get home, but now all he wanted was to crawl into bed and pretend that today hadn't happened. Colin and Jeremy sat in the backseat while Mrs. Rodson hummed happily. Colin listened as Jeremy launched into a one-sided conversation about Sam Bale and all the gossip he'd heard since the announcement. Other than offering a cursory "um-huh" and an occasional "yeah," Colin's mind remained firmly elsewhere with his many questions that not only weren't getting answered but were also gathering reinforcements.

My dreams.

The dreams from the previous night had something to do with people hunting him.

Or did it?

Giant hairy creatures in his shower?

Hallucinations maybe?

The goth twins.

Could be a virus?

And now the death of Sam Bale.

What next?

"So will you come out tonight then?" Jeremy whispered.

"What?" answered Colin, lost in his own thoughts.

"Were you listening to anything I said?"

"Every single word."

Jeremy glanced at his mom, but she too seemed caught up in her own musings. "I said that a few of us are going to head out to Merton Forest this evening and look at the crime scene," said Jeremy enthusiastically but quietly. "Do you want to come?"

Colin's stomach turned at the thought. "Why would you want to? What are you hoping to see?"

"I don't know. It's just something to do, ya know?"

"I'll pass."

"You're sure?"

"Certain."

"Suit yourself."

Mrs. Rodson pulled to a stop outside Colin's house. "Here you go, Colin," said Mrs. Rodson. "Sorry again about the little accident."

Colin nodded politely.

"Jer, do you ever find Elkwood a bit weird?" asked Colin.

"What do you mean?"

"I don't know. The people? The weather? It's just … don't you think it *feels* weird?"

Jeremy shook his head. "Nope. Seems normal to me."

Oblivious. Or maybe I'm just crazy.

Colin got out of the car. "All right, well, have fun tonight. Try not to get attacked by any wild dogs, wolves, or rabid rabbits."

Jeremy laughed. A tenth grader had come up with the theory that Sam Bale had been killed by a group of rabid rabbits. It got a few laughs.

***

Colin's grandmother was watching *Wheel of Fortune* as he passed the living room.

"Did you hear about that boy?" snapped his grandmother.

This was new. His grandmother rarely tried to make conversation. She normally just called him names and told him what a disappointment he was.

"Yeah, they let us out of school early because of it."

She didn't take her blind eyes off the TV. "Did you know him?"

"We had a few classes together." And even if he

hadn't, everyone knows everyone in Elkwood. The place wasn't big enough not to.

"Nasty business. I don't suppose you had anything to do with it?"

"With what, Grandma?"

"With his death." She turned toward him. Her blank eyes would send chills through a penguin, but there was something else there that Colin wasn't used to seeing. She looked sad.

"No, of course not! I ... I don't know anything."

The old lady turned back to the TV. "Good! I don't need any murderers living under my roof. Get yourself some food! You look unhealthy!"

This was familiar ground. He was used to her insults, and although he didn't need any more reasons to dislike himself, he still found it somewhat comforting.

Colin ate several cans of precooked spaghetti, a leftover container of mac and cheese, six slices of bread, two apples, and a frozen steak that he microwaved until it was hot enough to eat.

What is the deal with my appetite?

After drinking an entire jug of water, he cleared away the dishes and ran upstairs. It was just after 5:00 p.m., and thanks to the eternally overcast skies of Elkwood, it was already starting to get dark. Exhaustion washed over him, and his bed looked entirely too inviting. He stripped down to his underwear and didn't even bother trying to find some clean or at least semi-clean pyjamas. Flopping into bed, he rolled to look at the gray sky outside his window. Colin couldn't remember the last time the sun had shined in Elkwood.

Somewhere outside he could hear what sounded like a helicopter. A now familiar twinge signalled the oncoming headache that had accompanied too many strange events today. Colin buried his face in his pillow and tried to will it away. The whir of helicopter blades grew louder, and Colin's memory suffered a sudden seizure.

A radio play, Becca's dad, a helicopter, a creature, a car crash, biting, howling, explosion, pain!

The pain ripped through his body. Every muscle in his body felt like it was contracting and then pulsating, then contracting again. Sweat-slicked sheets bunched beneath his body as his back arched unnaturally. Vomit threatened the back of his throat, and his head pounded a relentless drumbeat that vibrated through his muscles and bones. And then, he passed out.

***

Fire drenched his dreams. Fire and screaming. A medieval town with thatched roofs and low-built stone homes where livestock used to wander the streets but now the carcasses of cattle, chickens, and sheep littered the dirt road that wound through the town. Men carrying swords and pitchforks surrounded Colin. He could smell fear everywhere. Fear and hate. It was such a strong, nauseating scent that Colin's head swam, barely able to focus. He looked down at his hands which turned out not to be hands at all. They were massive and covered with thick hair. Each finger tipped with a black, sharp claw.

Growling fiercely at the frightened faces of the townsfolk, he realized they meant him harm. He wouldn't give them the chance.

Unexpectedly Colin caught a scent in the air and felt a break in his dream. Like he was lying in his bed at home but at the same time still connected to the creature in the mediaeval town. He could smell Becca Emerson. She wasn't big on fragrances, and this wasn't one distinct smell like a perfume, but it was her. She smelled ... what was it?

Adventurous?

Colin, the creature, looked around, but his mind wasn't with the townsfolk anymore. A burly man with armor clearly too small for him screamed and threw a spear at Colin. The blade sliced through Colin's chest, and he roared in pain—

—sitting bolt upright in bed.

"Jesus! Colin!" yelped Becca. "You scared me!"

It was dark out. Colin was breathing heavily, covered in sweat and not much else. At the end of his bed stood Becca Emerson. She wore her usual dark clothing, heavy eye shadow, and held a flashlight in one of her gloved hands.

"I scared *you?* Becca, what are you doing in my bedroom?" Colin demanded.

Maybe I'm still dreaming?

"I came in the back door. You should really lock it."

"Yeah, good advice. What are you doing here?"

Colin looked at his clock. It was 1:00 a.m.

"I'm going to Merton Forest. Want to come?" She smelled excited.

How can someone smell excited?

It smelled like lavender and the color purple.

Colin blinked a few times to make sure he wasn't dreaming.

When the girl you've secretly been crushing on for the last year breaks into your house in the middle of the night, wakes you up, and asks you to visit the scene of a crime with her, what else do you say?

"Let me put on some pants."

Chapter Seven

Sniffing Around

The night was crisp and cool as they slipped out the same patio door through which Becca had secretly entered Colin's home. The fog was less dense than it had been during the day, which made navigating through town a lot easier. Not that it was really an issue as, not surprisingly, no one was out at 1:30 a.m. Colin had tried to think of something smart to say in hopes of impressing Becca but was failing miserably. His headache and general soreness had subsided but there were lingering scents from his dreams that disturbed him. Mostly the smells of fire and blood.

"Why are you so twitchy?" said Becca.

"I didn't realize I was."

"You're like a chihuahua."

"Cute with big ears?" Colin asked hopefully.

"They're always so jumpy."

Colin didn't know much about flirting but he was almost certain this wasn't it.

"Well if you had my grandmother, you'd be jumpy too."

Becca laughed, and Colin smiled triumphantly.

Ha! I made a funny.

"She is one seriously creepy old lady," said Becca.

"She comes from a long line of crypt keepers."

Becca laughed again, louder, and the sound bounced around empty buildings as they walked down Main Street.

I'm on fire!

"You should see her without the wig. Her head looks like a rotting avocado," Colin laughed.

"Ugh, Colin, that's just gross. How on earth did it look like a— Never mind, I don't want to know."

Colin shoved his hands in his pocket and decided to change the direction of conversation. "Why are we going to Merton Forest anyway? Any why did you wake me up? And how many times have you broken into people's houses?"

Becca counted her answers off on her fingers.

"To see the crime scene. Because I don't want to go by myself. And including tonight, five times."

"That was very ... truthful."

"I don't know if you've noticed, but I don't exactly have many good friends."

"I'm a good friend?" said Colin, immediately wishing he hadn't.

"If you have to ask, I guess not."

"Can I change my question?" he said quickly.

Becca glanced at Colin. "You're pretty sharp for someone who just woke up."

I am pretty sharp? I'm never sharp.

And he wasn't lying to himself either. Colin maintained average grades and didn't really excel at anything. *Sharp* was not a common word people used to describe him.

They reached the southern edge of town and hopped a wooden fence into a field.

"If we cut across the Merton Farm fields, it'll be quicker than taking the road around," said Becca, pulling a flashlight out of her pocket and switching it on. "What were you dreaming about?"

Colin was beginning to notice that Becca had a very disconcerting way of speaking. She had a habit of cutting to the chase. It freaked Colin out.

"What do you mean?"

"When I woke you up, you were covered in sweat and moaning."

"I was moaning?"

"Yeah, I was worried you were in pain."

Colin flushed and felt thankful that it was dark. "I've had some bad dreams lately. Along with some weird hunger cravings. And mild hallucinations. Oh, and headaches. It's all really strange."

"Well, you're in the right place. Elkwood is the place for strange."

"Does your dad know you're out tonight?"

"What do you think?"

"So no one knows we're out here?"

Becca stopped and gave Colin a coy smile. "What's

the matter, Colin? Afraid?"

"No, I'm not scared," countered Colin. "But there is supposed to be some sort of wild animal wandering around out here, you know."

Becca turned away from Colin and then without warning threw herself back at him. If this had happened yesterday, Colin would have dropped her but he easily caught her around the waist in his current state. Becca laid her head on his shoulder and peered up at him.

"That's why I brought you, my brave warrior," sighed Becca dramatically. "To protect me against the evil beasty." Smiling, she stood up and laughed.

"Don't mock me!" said Colin. "I mean, it's funny, but still."

Becca carried on walking with Colin dutifully following. "I like that you can take a joke, Colin."

"You won't find it so funny when you're being torn to shreds by some creature and I'm already halfway back to town."

"You wouldn't do that."

"You're right. I'd be too scared to move."

They both laughed. Colin felt happier than he had in a long time. And that worried him. He'd always been under the impression that he wasn't allowed to be happy.

"So what are you hoping to find at the crime scene?" said Colin.

"I don't know. I figured you'd be more curious than me."

"Why?"

"One of our classmates gets attacked by a wild animal the same night that you're out driving around town in what I can only assume was a stolen vehicle."

There it was. Did Becca think Colin had killed Sam Bale?

"You were out too," said Colin, probably a little too defensively.

"Then this is a good way to clear both our names. Why were you out last night anyway?"

"Why were you out?" he countered.

"Touché, Mr. Strauss," said Becca. "Don't worry, Colin. I don't think you're a wild animal nor do I believe that any fiber of your being has the ability to attack anyone, let alone kill them."

"I guess that makes you the prime suspect then," said Colin jokingly. Becca punched him in the shoulder playfully. "See! Violent offender right here!" shouted Colin.

"Shush."

They had crossed several fields and hopped a number of fences, catching glimpses of the flickering light from the Merton farmhouse in the distance. The moon should have been full tonight but the overcast sky hid any evidence of it. As they walked downhill toward the forest, the open fields weren't as well tended the farther away from the farmhouse they went, making walking a bit of a hazard.

As they walked, Colin tried to keep from dwelling on the flashes from his disturbing dream, but they refused to stay down in the dark corners of his mind. This was his first happy moment in a long time, and he didn't want to ruin it by contemplating whatever was going on with his mind and body.

"Colin, how can you possibly see where you're going?"

Lost in thought, Colin hadn't realized that he'd started drifting from Becca who was following the light from her flashlight. The grass was long and spotted with spiny shrubs, but Colin could make everything out just fine.

"I have good night vision?"

"You have amazing night vision. Can you see the forest?"

To Colin's surprise, he could. The far edge of the field they had entered ended in a bank of trees that stretched off in either direction. "Yes, it's at the end of this field."

"That's amazing. Have you always been able to do that?"

"Uh, no ... well, yeah."

"I love a straight answer, Colin."

As they made their way across the field, Colin weaved easily to avoid shrubs, and Becca carefully picked her way through and still occasionally got tangled. Colin could make something out toward the west. He could just see an open area at the edge of the forest, surrounded by four large yet dark floodlights.

"Look over there."

"Colin, I can barely see my hand in front of my face."

"It's the crime scene. Come on."

Colin grabbed Becca's hand and led her through the field in the right direction. Reaching the caution tape, Colin hesitated. He'd seen cop shows; you weren't supposed to do this. It was wrong. It was illegal. The tape was bright yellow with big words that read *caution* for a good reason.

Becca ducked under the tape and began scanning the area with her flashlight.

Maybe she doesn't watch TV?

Colin threw caution to the wind and entered the crime scene. It was weird to think he was standing close to where someone he knew, or at least someone who had beaten him up, had died.

The fog was very light in the clearing, almost nonexistent. The clouds began to break, and Colin could see the moon. The same uncomfortable sensation that had preceded his earlier migraines began to creep up his spine. *Oh no. Not now!*

His body no longer fit easily inside his skin, and his muscles began to tense. Until ... it stopped.

The crime scene exploded in a wave of clarity as Colin breathed deeply through his nose. He could pinpoint the location of the attack, easily picking out where all the blood spatters converged in one place. There was a trail of blood where Sam must have been dragged into the trees. Colin could literally see the blood ... or smell it? He couldn't decide. All he knew was that he could perceive everything in bright vibrant washes of color, in the dark without a flashlight.

The world wasn't dark to him. He could see Becca examining the area with a flashlight. She looked beautiful. Colin could hear her heart beating like a drum. And he could smell her, her happiness at being out at night and doing something she probably shouldn't be.

Faintly, Colin caught a whiff of something else. Another smell. Familiar, but ... not good. Something dangerous.

"It looks like they cleaned everything up. I don't see anything," said Becca. "How about you? Picking anything up with your super night vision?" She smiled and shone the flashlight directly into his face. She looked surprised. "Colin, what's wrong with your eyes? They're—"

"Becca Emerson and Colin Strauss. What are you two doing here?" Colin and Becca jumped as Gareth Dugan marched out of the forest carrying a flashlight. Colin could smell waves of anger coming from him.

"Gareth, what are you doing here?" said Becca.

"Interesting pairing. Would never have guessed you were into the dark and brooding type, Colin. But then I wouldn't have though that you'd be into the weak loser type either, Becca."

"Gareth, you're an idiot," said Becca.

"That's your opinion. And it's wrong."

Something about Gareth was off. Way off. He didn't smell completely human, although Colin couldn't necessarily tell what human smelled like. He just knew there was something unnatural about Gareth. As if there was something lurking under the surface.

What if he's the killer? What if he's the animal that killed Sam Bale?

"Did you kill Sam, Gareth?" blurted Colin.

"Colin!" said Becca.

"It's not completely outside the realm of possibility, Becca."

Gareth looked sad. "Don't be an idiot, Colin. Sam was my friend."

"Then what are you doing out here?"

Gareth bristled at Colin's question. "What am I

doing out here? What are you two doing out here?"

"Becca wanted to look around."

"So you just followed her like a lovesick puppy. Ha!"

"Well, it wasn't exactly like that."

"It was kind of like that." Becca shrugged.

"Oh, this is great. Becca and Colin. I'm going to throw up."

Something about the crime scene continued to nag at Colin.

Why floodlights?

Sam's body had been discovered during the day. What are the lights for? Suddenly, he caught it, just the lightest whiff on the breeze, the smell of other people. Several other people. The distant sound of a helicopter.

Colin heard the whir of a generator as it powered up. The floodlights burst to life illuminating the crime scene and three startled teenagers.

"Run!" yelled Becca.

Colin didn't know what to do. He froze as his migraine came back full force. The smells, the sounds, the light, and then the helicopter coming closer all blinded his senses. He tried to stagger in the general direction Becca was running.

"Come on, Colin!" she shouted.

He mind recalled the explosion, a helicopter, and running through the forest, but most of all, he remembered the wolf creature. He heard it growl inside his head.

In an eerie human voice, it said, "I'll take it from here."

Colin blacked out.

***

As his vision returned, Colin realized he was standing next to the wooden fence at the southern edge of town where he and Becca had first crossed into the field. There was a commotion far behind him somewhere.

"Colin, put me down!" said Becca

Colin realized he had Becca slung over his shoulder. He put her down. "What? How ...?" said Colin.

"That's what I'd like to know," demanded Becca. "Come on. We need to hide for a while."

"My grandfather's garage is only a couple of blocks away."

"Let's go. Then you can explain to me exactly what just happened."

What did just happen?

Chapter Eight

Recollections

Colin found it unusual that he was in the same back alley, breaking into his grandfather's garage again, two nights in a row. He didn't have the key for the back door this time, but Becca found a window that was unlocked. Colin helped her through the window, and she unlocked the door from the inside.

The garage was exactly as it had been the night before, minus one car. That must mean he definitely did steal it last night. He just wished he could fully remember what had happened.

Colin's grandfather had kept an old oil-stained couch in the back of the shop. Becca flopped down and patted the couch playfully. "Here, boy!" she said.

Colin hesitated.

"I don't bite, Colin. And you can't tell me that you're not tired after what just happened."

Colin sat down carefully beside her. "Yeah, about that. I can't really remember—"

"Oh, come on, Colin! It just happened! How can you not remember?"

"Well, my memory ... it's been a little, well, off lately."

"You're telling me that you can't remember what just happened out in the field?"

"Nope."

"You're full of crap."

"Do you interrogate often? Isn't there supposed to be a *good* cop to balance out your surly no-nonsense attitude?"

Becca smiled, punching him good-naturedly in the shoulder.

"Hey! Police brutality!"

"All right," said Becca patiently. "Let's take a deep breath and try to trace our way backwards. Maybe it'll jog your memory and then you can explain how you did that."

"That all sounds very complicated, but I'll do my best," Colin smiled.

"What's the last thing you remember?"

Colin thought back to the field. It was like trying to see through fog. "I remember the crime scene."

"That's a start. What else?"

"I remember Gareth Dugan."

"And then?" Becca prompted.

"And then ... nothing. The next thing I remember is being at the edge of town with you slung over my shoulder."

"What about the floodlights? Do you remember the lights coming on?"

Colin could feel the migraine skipping along the edges of his brain. It was blocking his memories, threatening to return.

But they're my memories!

He could recall the lights coming on. "I remember the lights!"

The migraine seemed to stop skipping and backed away a little.

Colin continued as bits and pieces slipped back. "I remember Gareth turning and running back into the woods. There was a gunshot. Did Gareth get shot?"

"I don't know; you'd already grabbed me by that point."

"Grabbed you?"

"Yes, Colin, you grabbed me, threw me over your shoulder like I was nothing, and then raced off across the field."

Colin thought his school bag was heavy. Picking up an actual person had never struck him as being a good idea.

"I've never seen anyone move like that. You're a lot stronger than you look," said Becca.

"I get that a lot."

I never get that.

"Why were the cops staking out the crime scene?" wondered Colin.

"I don't think it was necessarily cops."

"Then who was—"

Becca pulled a buzzing phone from her pocket. She

read something on the screen and stood. "I have to go."

"Now? But we don't even know what just happened? Or why? Or with who?"

"It's my dad, it's an emergency, and it's too hard to explain. I'll call you tomorrow."

Colin stood up. He looked down at Becca.

Am I ... getting taller?

"Well, thanks for an eventful night," said Colin because, frankly, he didn't know what else to say at this point.

Becca smiled. "Thanks for getting out of bed." She kissed Colin on the cheek, and a strange look came across her face.

"What's the matter?"

"I don't know. There's something different about you. Something's changed."

"I'm not wearing deodorant."

"I'm being serious. You ... tomorrow. We'll talk about it tomorrow." Becca absentmindedly touched her lips and then turned and left the garage.

Colin stood alone next to the old couch and thought about how much of an idiot he was. He was having blackouts, hallucinations, students were getting torn to pieces and possibly shot, he'd lost his grandfather's car. It was all very serious stuff. The thing that really stood out for him was one single thought.

Becca Emerson just kissed me.

Realizing it was 3:30 a.m., he locked the garage door and climbed back out through the window, dropping to the alley floor with ease.

He didn't see the large piece of wood that broke

across his head or the person who swung it. The last thing Colin remembered before passing out (again) was being dragged down the alley dreamily thinking one single thought: *Becca Emerson kissed me.*

Idiot.

***

When Colin woke up, he was chained to a heavy chair in a dark basement. Water dripped from pipes that ran along the ceiling. He'd seen this sort of scene in a movie once. He wasn't a fan of horror flicks, but he knew that it usually didn't end well for the teenager chained to the chair.

The only illumination came from a portable light hanging from one of the pipes above Colin's head. Despite the darkness, he found he could see fairly well. He sniffed the air and caught a familiar scent. Not a normal thing to do, but it felt right.

As he inhaled, pieces of the room looked brighter, clearer to him. Colin could smell gas, and sure enough, there were several cans stacked in a corner. There were other things: the smell of fresh timber coming from a stack of wood, paint from an open paint can, and something else. He sniffed hard, and there it was again. The smell from his dreams, the smell from the man in the fog yesterday. Making that connection, Colin could suddenly see the man. He was standing in the darkest corner of the basement watching Colin intently. It was definitely the same man. He was wearing a long jacket with a hood, but Colin couldn't make out his face.

"Who are you?" said Colin.

"Who are you?" echoed the man. The voice was the same gruff rasp from his dreams. It was a vague memory, but he remembered it.

"I'm Colin."

"And how are you feeling today, Colin?"

"Tired. It's been a strange couple of days."

"Do you know what's happening to you, Colin?"

"I'm chained to a chair?"

The man had wrapped chains around Colin's arms, legs, and upper body; only his head was free. What struck Colin as strange was that his head didn't hurt in the slightest. He remembered getting hit with something heavy.

Maybe I'm in shock.

"You're not in shock, Colin."

"Did I say that? Or did I think it?"

"You thought it. And then I heard it," clarified the man unhelpfully.

"What are you going to do to me?"

"I think I've done my worst already." Sighing heavily, the man walked out of the shadows. Colin recognized him from his dreams. He looked to be in his late forties with light brown eyes and a muscular build. His hair was dark and greasy. "You don't need to be afraid of me, Colin."

"You've got to admit," said Colin, "there's currently not a lot of evidence to back up that statement. I mean, I am strapped to a chair in a dark basement."

The man smiled and dragged a folding chair in front of Colin and sat down. "My name is Silas Baxter. Do you know who I am?"

"Yeah, you just told me. You're Silas Baxter."

"Not my name, dummy. Do you know what I do?"

Colin remembered the dreams again. "You hunt people."

"Ah," nodded Silas. "So you've had the dreams already."

"What do you know about my dreams?"

"I know everything about you, Colin. I know that you've been moved from one family member to another since you were born. I know you live with your grandmother, and that you're miserable 95% of the time. I know that you ran away from home two nights ago and now you're having weird dreams and that your body is going through changes."

"How could you possibly know all this? It's impossible."

"I know that you have a tiny scar on your knee from when you fell off the monkey bars in fourth grade. The monkey bars were painted blue."

"That's very specific."

"It's funny what you remember. Most people can't remember what they ate for dinner last night, but they can remember the stuffed toy they went to sleep with when they were a kid."

"Mr. Snuffles," said Colin.

"He was a pink elephant."

"He was light red! And how do you know all this?"

"I know all this because you know all this. I've known

all this since I bit you the other night."

The explosion. The car crash. The werewolf.

"You! You were ... you are a werewolf!"

Colin felt stupid saying it aloud, but in his current situation, he figured it couldn't make matters any worse.

"In turn," said Silas, "you now know all about me. Not only me, but the entire blood strain of werewolf that courses through my veins. Or rather, our veins."

Colin struggled to make sense of his words "Am I going to turn into one of those things? Into a werewolf? It sounds stupid that I'm even saying this. Werewolf."

"There are all sorts of things that go bump in the night, Colin."

"Great. That's great. So now I'll be spending my life going bump in the night too? That wasn't really one of my career goals."

"You don't have any career goals."

"Stay out of my head!"

"I can't. You and I are connected. Forever."

"Why did you bite me? Why can't I hear your thoughts? In the dreams, you kill werewolves. Does that mean you're going to kill me?"

Colin was breathing heavily, and his vision was turning foggy. The dark parts of the basement swam in color as scents washed over him in waves. Somewhere close by—it may as well have been in the same room for how clear it sounded—he heard a cow *moo*.

Silas placed a large hand on Colin's shoulder. "Calm down, Colin. This is all perfectly normal."

Colin laughed like a crazy person.

Normal?

The smells subsided again, and he took deep breaths.

"Well, no. Not normal in the conventional sense," conceded Silas. "But if you're changing into a werewolf, then what you're going through is perfectly acceptable. Yes, you could have picked a better town than Elkwood. This isn't the best place for werewolves, you know."

"Did you kill Sam Bale?"

"No"

"Did I kill Sam Bale?"

"I don't know."

"Can't you just read my mind and find out?"

"I can't read your subconscious. The night that boy was killed was the same night I bit you. You probably don't remember anything after that."

"Just bits and pieces. I think I killed a deer." Colin felt nauseous and hungry all at the same time. "I ate a deer."

"When I bit you, it forced your body into an immediate change. Normally it doesn't happen like that."

"Oh, great. So I'm a weird werewolf?"

"It's not unheard of. It's just uncommon. Usually your body will change slowly towards the next lunar cycle, but yours is becoming erratic. Your visions, the hallucinations, they're all fairly rare."

"Rarer than a werewolf?"

"Good point," admitted Silas.

"If you hunt other werewolves, are you hunting me?"

"Maybe."

The cold sincerity with which Silas said the word gave Colin chills. "I don't know that you're not the werewolf that killed that boy. I had to run clear across the county last night before managing to lose the people chasing me," said Silas. "I tracked a werewolf here from California. The wolf I tracked is new, but he's already killed several times. I tracked him along the coast to Elkwood. I was closing in on his scent last night near the town hall when I was attacked and pursued by that team of operatives. That's when I ran into you and bit you."

"Yeah, about that biting thing. Why did you bite me again?"

Silas smelled embarrassed. It smelled like citrus, like a freshly cut orange. "I'd heard rumors of a town like Elkwood, but I didn't realize one actually existed. I thought I was going to be captured or killed, and I wanted to preserve my bloodline. What I do, the reasons I do it, I needed to pass that on. It was sheer luck that you were there."

"Yeah. Lucky me." Colin squirmed in his chains; there was no give at all. "What do you mean by *a town like Elkwood*. And operatives? And who's this other werewolf?"

Silas looked confused.

"You don't know what this place is? Colin, Elkwood is a—"

Silas looked past Colin.

"Elkwood is a what? Hello? Silas?"

"Do you hear that?"

"I don't hear—"

"Shh! Listen. Forget everything else and listen hard. Focus behind you."

Colin listened. He heard Silas's rapid heartbeat. The house was creaking as the wind lightly blew outside.

Cows mooing. He strained to hear beyond that but—

It came at him in a deafening rush. Vehicles! At least two of them. A mix of voices over the static of a radio sliced through his hearing.

"The Baker farm," said a female voice.

"Lights—"

"—weapons ready," confirmed a male.

"We have to go," whispered Silas. "Now." Colin's ears rang.

He grabbed the chains holding Colin to the chair and ripped them apart. Links bounced and clinked across the concrete floor. Colin just sat there trying to process the strength it would take to rip a chain apart like that as Silas did the same thing to the restraints around his legs. Silas grabbed Colin by the shirt and pulled him to his feet.

"Follow me," said Silas.

Colin followed him up the stairs and out of the basement. Colin found he could see quite clearly despite the dark. The smell of building materials was strong as the pair passed from one room to another. Colin realized the voice on the radio was correct; they were at the Baker farm. The Bakers were living in a small cottage at the other end of their property while this farmhouse was being renovated. Silas pulled Colin into a crouch in the living room, and crawled quickly toward the large bay window. Peering over the window ledge, Colin didn't need to be able to see in the dark to make out two sets of headlights bouncing down the long dirt driveway toward the house.

"They're looking for me," said both Colin and Silas at the same time.

"They're not looking for you, Colin. They don't even

know you're a threat. They've had some sort of psychic or mind reader tracking me."

Colin didn't want to bring up the events of the evening at the crime scene. Things were confusing enough as it was.

"Listen," said Silas. "I'll head toward the coastline and lead them away. You head out the back, move fast, stay low, and get back to town."

"And then what?"

"I'll be watching you."

"Because I might be a killer dog?"

"Yes, but I created you, which makes you my responsibility. I'll find you again. You're going to notice more changes as your human and wolf sides balance out. Best stay indoors whenever you can. Ignore the urges as much as possible! Go, now!"

Silas pushed Colin up.

"Urges? What urges? Who are these people who are chasing you? What's so special about Elkwood? How come—"

Colin turned around, but Silas had already left the room. The vehicles were through the main gate and fifty feet from the house. Colin turned and ran through the house. He grabbed the kitchen doorknob and yanked the entire door off its hinges.

Smells wafted at him, mostly from cows. He jumped from the back deck and hit the ground running. Somewhere behind him, car doors opened and closed, people shouting, but Colin didn't look back. He just kept running.

Half a mile later, he remembered to drop the kitchen door.

Chapter Nine

Suspicion

Colin had trouble sleeping. Strangely enough, it wasn't the knowledge that he was turning into a bloodthirsty creature or any of the other bizarre events from the last few days. It wasn't any of those things that kept him tossing and turning. It was the smells. Every time he drifted off, he'd catch a whiff of something in his room: a shoe, a dried ketchup stain, his laundry, books, the carpet, the remains of last week's grilled cheese sandwich. Every time a new scent floated to him, it was like getting slapped in the face.

Just before dawn, he finally dropped off to sleep for a couple of hours. He woke up when a smell of cheap hand cream and old lady perfume almost made his eyes water. His grandmother was standing over his bed staring at him. Or, at least, in his general direction.

Colin made a *grafaahh* sort of sound and pulled his blankets up to his neck. There are some things that you don't want to wake up to. His grandmother was one of those things.

"The police are here," said his grandmother.

"What?" Colin was instantly awake.

"They want to talk to you."

"About what?"

"Where were you last night?" She squinted her blind eyes, and Colin imagined she was examining his soul. He always felt like that when she was focused on him.

A crime scene, Grandfather's garage, chained up in the basement of the Baker's farmhouse.

"I was here, in bed, all night," claimed Colin hastily.

"Hmm. Some kids went to the crime scene last night. Made a mess. They're talking to kids from your class. You better not have been involved!"

"I wasn't. I was asleep, all night."

"I don't want to be harboring a criminal!"

"Oh, give it a rest!"

What am I doing?

Colin had never spoken to his grandmother like that. She was far too terrifying for that sort of rebellion. For a moment, she didn't say anything. She just fixed on him as if weighing him up, like a cobra giving serious thought to eating a mouse.

"Watch your tongue, young man, or you'll find yourself losing it," she said finally. "Get some clothes on. Those police men are taking up space in my living room, and I want to watch *The Price is Right*."

The old lady shuffled out of Colin's room, slamming the door behind her. Colin rubbed his temples and tried to compose himself. He slipped on some jeans and a

T-shirt and went to leave his room, but his reflection gave him pause.

He looked bigger. All over. Like he'd swollen overnight. His hair looked thicker, and his eyes were …

Brighter?

He moved closer to the mirror. Colin hadn't grown any facial hair yet. Still, he'd tried shaving the nothingness on his face to encourage growth. It didn't work. Staring back at him now, however, was a face with the lightest shadow of hair as if he'd been shaving for years. His complexion was completely clear, and his face looked full of life, less pale. Even his overall lankiness had been eaten up by broader shoulders and upper body definition. He pulled up his shirt.

I have muscles!

There was a definition to his stomach that hadn't been there before. His chest seemed more pronounced.

Silas had told him that the human and wolf inside him were trying to balance out. Would he wake up one morning to find himself completely covered in hair? Did he even care?

I look amazing!

He admired himself in the mirror again.

"Colin Strauss, get down here right now," came the shrill shriek of his grandmother from downstairs.

Colin ran down the stairs taking two at a time. His grandmother was sitting in her chair with an angry look on her face. In her defense, it was the exact same look that she always had.

Colin recognized the two police officers. One was Sherriff Drewbaker, a tiny, older gentleman with bug eyes and a distinctly weathered look. The other was a deputy Colin had seen around town but didn't know by name.

"Good morning, Colin," said the sheriff. "This here is Deputy Grint. We'd like to ask you a few questions."

Colin's stomach twisted in knots, and he started sweating.

"You two want a cup of coffee?" asked his grandmother.

"No, ma'am, thank you," said the sheriff.

"Good," said his grandmother. "Now get on with it. I'm sure you have better things to do in this town than harass my grandson. He's a good boy!"

Well, this is different.

In Colin's entire history of life, he couldn't recall his grandmother ever referring to him as *good*. Lazy? Yes. Good-for-nothing? Absolutely. Waste of space? On several occasions.

"Of course, we won't take up much of your time," said the sheriff. "Now, Colin, you obviously know about the incident with Sam Bale?"

Colin nodded.

Small movements, Colin, nothing too abrupt and don't do anything that makes you look guilty.

"Eaten by a wolf?" blurted out Colin.

The sheriff and Deputy Grint looked at Colin. Deputy Grint adjusted his belt.

What did I just say?

"Well," said the Sheriff, "there are a lot of wild rumors floating around. Something attacked and killed him, but we don't know what yet. We're still waiting on forensics."

"Probably a bobcat," declared his grandmother.

"That's a possibility," continued the sheriff. "Colin,

I'll get to the point. There were some kids who went out to the crime scene last night. With this sort of crime, it's important to preserve the area until we can evaluate all the evidence. We don't want people wandering around out there, especially since we don't know what kind of animal we're dealing with."

"I was in bed all night." Colin interrupted so quickly that it sounded more like *Iwasinbedallnight*.

"So you never went out last night? Maybe with your friend Jeremy?"

"Jeremy? No, I never saw Jeremy last night. I was in bed all night. He wasn't in bed with me. I mean, I was alone all night."

"You seem nervous, Mr. Strauss," observed Deputy Grint, adjusting his belt again.

Yeah, I might have eaten Sam Bale. You'd be nervous too.

"No, I'm fine. I'm good, really quite good. Are you guys okay?"

The sheriff sighed. "Are you sure there's nothing you want to tell us, Colin?"

"Nope," said Colin, this time too slowly.

The sheriff and Deputy Grint stared at him.

What are they waiting for? Am I supposed to say something else? Man, I feel hungry.

And he did. An overwhelming hunger washed over him as if he'd been lost in the desert for two weeks and just found a McDonald's. The room shifted slightly as Colin's senses kicked into overdrive. Suddenly very aware of his surroundings, he could hear an irritating, high-pitched whine.

"You guys hear that? Is that the TV?"

The sound melted into the background as details from the fading yellow wallpaper in his grandmother's living room jumped into view. The layers of color on the TV set were so distinctly clear. He could see the individual hairs in the creepy moustache of Deputy Grint. Turning slightly, he noticed the skin on the sheriff's arms. He wanted to bite it. He wanted to bite the sheriff's arm right off and feel his teeth sink into the sinewy flesh and muscle, feel the warm blood trickle down his chin, and—

"Colin, are you okay?" asked the sheriff warily. "Your eyes are a little ... wide."

Colin's senses still blared at him, but he managed a small nod. He had the feeling that if he tried to open his mouth he'd end up trying to eat Elkwood's sheriff.

"Okay, boys. I think it's time for you to go," said Colin's grandmother, suddenly standing between Colin and the two policemen.

"We're almost done here," said Deputy Grint.

"Are you sure, young man?" asked the little old lady. "Are you sure you're not done now?"

Thunder rumbled somewhere in the distance as another storm began to boil over Elkwood.

"Look here, Mrs—"

The sheriff put a hand on Deputy Grint's shoulder. It was a small movement, but Colin watched as the sheriff gave a small shake of his head toward his deputy.

"Yes, we're done now. Thank you, ma'am," said the sheriff. Both men left quickly. Grint smelled angry to Colin, like a campfire that had just been doused with water.

As soon as the front door closed all ninety pounds

of Colin's grandmother swivelled around and fixed her blind eyes on Colin's face.

"You lied to those men. You're hiding something."

"I don't feel well," blurted Colin. "I think I'm coming down with something."

Like werewolf-itis.

"Then you best get to bed. I don't want any sickness in this house. Get up those stairs and get some rest, and whatever you're hiding, whatever you didn't tell those men, it better not be anything serious."

Colin turned and headed upstairs, his senses still bouncing around wildly. The rain continued to fall on the street outside, and sounds drifted from the neighbors' houses. He heard his grandmother shuffle back into the living room and the creak of her old chair as she settled into it. Then she began talking to herself.

"Gallivanting around wet fields in the middle of the night with some girl is a sure recipe for sickness if you ask me," muttered his grandmother.

How did she know?

Colin really was tired. His whole body felt heavier. He crawled back into bed but couldn't get comfortable. After much repositioning, he finally curled up into a ball at the bottom of his bed and drifted off to sleep.

Chapter Ten

Sleeping Wolf

I. Am. A. Werewolf.

This was the first thought that came to mind every time he awoke that restless night. In an effort to get some sleep, Colin finally figured out if he smelled something once, it wouldn't be strong enough to wake him up. He began systematically sniffing his entire room. He started at the corner near the window and moved around counter clockwise until he was back at his bed and confident that he'd inventoried every scent in his room.

Will I have to do this every night? Or at least on the nights when I'm not out eating my classmates.

He crawled back into his bed, tried to get comfy the conventional way but failed and ended up curling up in a ball at the end of his bed again. In an instant, he was asleep and dreaming of angry townsfolk hunting him through dark forests once more. Distantly he heard

Silas calling his name, but he was too preoccupied with avoiding the mob to answer.

***

Colin awoke to several smells all centered around one thing. Crushed lavender, cheap skin cream, anger, frustration, worry ... and something else he couldn't place. It wasn't an object, and his newly sensitized nose couldn't identify it as anything emotional; it was just ... something.

Without opening his eyes, Colin mumbled, "Good morning, Grandmother."

"Hmph! Morning, is it? You've been asleep almost twenty-four hours, you lazy little ingrate!" said his grandmother.

Colin opened his eyes, breathing in the scent of rain on the wet concrete outside only to find his diminutive grandmother towering over his bed, attention fixed on his prone form. "It's Sunday?" said Colin.

"Yes. You should get out and get some fresh air. It'll do you good!"

"Okay, I'm moving, I'm moving."

Apparently satisfied, she shuffled out of Colin's room.

Colin sat up and rubbed his face with his hands, clearing the sleep away. What he encountered was far from usual. Scrambling over to the mirror, he was met with a changed reflection. His body had become even more defined, still lanky but far more angular than before. Strangely enough, that wasn't the weird part.

I have hair!

Colin had the kind of hair that a Canadian lumberjack would be proud of. The hair on his head felt thicker, and he had a beard! Okay, not a beard. But he definitely had a thicker shadow. Pulling his T-shirt off, Colin noticed definite muscle definition. If this is what being a werewolf meant, maybe he could overlook the eating people thing.

Loser. You can't eat people.

Colin still had so many questions. What did Silas know about Elkwood? Why did the twins throw up in class? Why was the crime scene being staked out? Who were the people hunting Silas? Where was the other werewolf Silas had been tracking? Why did Becca—

Becca!

He'd completely forgotten about her. She had said they would talk yesterday. Had she called while he was asleep?

Colin rummaged around in his desk drawer and pulled out an old flip cell phone that might have been popular in the late nineties. He didn't carry it with him for fear of embarrassment, and no one ever called him anyway. It was pre-paid, however, so he could at least use it without his grandmother listening in. He flipped open his laptop and searched for the Emerson's number, punched in the digits and waited.

"Hello," answered a male voice. Colin assumed Mr. Emerson.

"Uh, is Becca there?"

"Who is this?"

"Mr. Emerson?" asked Colin.

"That's who I am. Who are you?"

"Oh, sorry, Mr. Emerson. This is Colin Strauss. I was wondering if Becca was home."

"The Strauss boy. Hang on a moment."

Like he was standing in the room with him, Colin heard Mr. Emerson sit down in a chair, maybe leather, and type at a computer; someone else in the room shifted their weight and took a drink of something.

Mr. Emerson whispered under his breath, "Ordinary."

"Mr. Emerson?"

"I'm sorry, Colin, but Becca isn't feeling well today. She's resting."

"Is she okay?"

"I'm sure it's nothing. Thanks for calling."

"Could you let her know I—"

But he'd already hung up.

Ordinary?

Colin stuck the phone in his pocket; maybe he'd try again later. He pulled on a shirt and jeans and wondered whether he should shave. He knew nothing about being a werewolf. A few Google searches showed that the Internet didn't have a clue either. Lots of speculation and stories about vicious mythical beasts that terrorized villages, stole livestock, and tore people limb from limb. He found some information about a European cult that worshipped wolf-like creatures, and there was a ton of North American mythology centered on people turning into werewolves, but nothing really useful. What he really needed was to speak to Silas Baxter.

He pulled on a sweater and rain jacket and headed downstairs. His grandmother was asleep in her chair, so Colin tiptoed into the kitchen and ate two bowls of cereal and some leftover pasta. Still hungry unwilling to hang around long enough for the old bat to wake up, Colin stepped out of the house into the pounding rain.

Colin felt anxious but couldn't figure out why. Knowing he wanted to find Silas Baxter, he decided to head for the Baker farm, hoping Silas would still be around. Maybe he could sense him? Smell him? Anything was worth trying at this point.

He set off walking, his runners getting damper with every step. There it was again, that anxious feeling. Then it came to him.

Walking is too slow! I want to run!

The thought had barely crossed his mind before he was sprinting down the street. It felt good!

He ran fast, faster than ever before, faster than most Olympic athletes. The streets were quiet, but Colin didn't want to attract attention. He headed out of town and then broke south before the city limits, hopping over the stone walls that separated the farm fields, sprinting across the rolling grassy hills, never losing pace. His world melted into a blur, and Colin lost himself in the simplicity of running, his worries disappearing as he ran.

Every time he jumped a wall, he felt like he could go higher. Increasing his speed, his feet thundering across the ground, he crouched before reaching the next fence and threw himself up with all his might. Colin flew into the air, ten, twenty, thirty feet and landed lightly in the middle of the next field, knees bent to absorb the impact. He stood up slowly.

I'm strong. And fast. I've never been strong or fast.

He felt amazing, and it wasn't just his newfound strength or speed. Every raindrop, every blade of grass, was crystal clear, and the smells! The smell of the earth, the trees, the rocks. He wanted to roll in the fields and take it all in.

I have to find Silas.

Recalling his purpose, he took off at a run again. Five minutes later, the Baker farm came into view with two memorable black cars parked nearby. Colin ducked behind one of the field walls and peeked over. The perimeter of the house had been cordoned off with yellow warning tape. There was no chance of Silas being there, and Colin wasn't willing to get any closer. Not with those people hanging around.

His cell phone chirped. Colin flipped it open.

"Hello," breathed Colin.

"Colin, you're okay?"

It was Becca; she sounded tired. Maybe even sick. He could hear her heartbeat through the phone. It was slow.

"Am I okay? Are you okay? You don't sound good. Not that you're not good, I'm sure you're fine. I don't know what I'm saying."

Becca laughed weakly. "You do sound like you. I'm fine, just tired. I'm sorry I didn't call you. It ended up being a busy weekend."

"That's okay. I was busy catching up on my sleep. The police did drop by yesterday though, wanting to know if I'd been out at the crime scene."

"What did you tell them?"

"I told them to get out of my house and to go chase a donut."

"You did not."

"No, I didn't. I told them I was in bed the whole time. I got the impression they were questioning everyone. Did they visit you?"

"No. But I'm the farthest thing from a criminal."

"Says the girl who breaks into people's houses in the middle of the night."

Becca laughed again. "Are you going to the memorial service for Sam Bale today?"

"I didn't even know it was today. I wasn't planning on it. You?"

"No. Need to rest up before school tomorrow. I should let you go. You're probably busy."

"It's true, I'm planning my next crime. This interruption is going to set me back a ways."

"All right, evil genius. I'll see you tomorrow. Try to stay out of trouble."

"I'll do my best."

"Bye.

And she was gone. Colin was getting good at this talking to girls stuff. He peeked over the wall again as a black van pulled in the drive, joining the two black cars already there. Colin watched as two men in hazmat suits got out of the van and entered the house.

Who are these guys?

The high-pitched, whining sound ripped through his skull again, but it unexpectedly morphed into a dull drone, finally settling into fuzziness, like static in the background. Colin dropped down behind the wall and closed his eyes. Why did this keep happening? Was his werewolf-sense kicking in again?

Ha! Werewolf-sense.

That's a stupid name, said the voice of Silas Baxter inside Colin's head.

"Silas?"

Colin, can you hear me?

"Yes, I can hear you. Where are you?"

Colin, are you there? Hello?

"I can hear you loud and clear."

You idiot, I can't hear you because you're talking out loud, aren't you?

What?

I knew it. Remember, I said we're connected? Your gifts are developing, but your change is erratic. It'll come and go. Sometimes you might even hear other people's thoughts, or they might hear yours. You and I can communicate this way. Until you've gone through your first real change, it's probably not going to work all the ...

Silas?

What?

You cut off.

I told you it won't work all the time.

So we can think to each other, just like this? You can hear my thoughts, I can hear yours?

Yes.

So anything I think of, you'll know.

Yes, anything.

Anything at all?

Yes, Colin, even when you think about girls.

Don't think about girls, don't think about girls.

I can still hear you.

It seems like this sort of arrangement wouldn't give either of us much privacy?

It's part of being a werewolf. I bit you, so now we're a pack.

A pack of two?

Still a pack.

Unless you have to kill me?

That's right.

Well as long as we're on the same page.

Where are you?

I came back to the Baker farm looking for you.

You're at the Baker farm?

Yeah, those people are still here.

Get the hell out of there, Colin! Get far away fast!

Colin was running before he gave it any real thought.

This is why I was looking for you. Who are these people? What's going to happen to me next? What's so special about Elkwood? Who is the other werewolf you came here to hunt? When are we ... Silas?

Colin effortlessly cleared the next wall with a long leap and continued running.

Keep ... low profile. B ... sure t ... shave. Will contact whe ... able. R ... mber, kee ... low profile.

Silas? Come in, Silas?

Nothing. His brain was back to being as empty as always.

With Silas's warning he realized, he hadn't fully considered the ramifications of his hair growing abnormally. People would surely notice at school tomorrow.

Colin changed his course, heading south so he could

slip over to the corner store/gas station/tire centre/hair emporium to pick up some shaving supplies.

Lost in thought, Colin caught the sound of a droning voice and the smell of sadness. It was hard to describe how he knew it was sadness, but it smelled like a large room with nothing in it.

Standing at the edge of the vast Elkwood Cemetery, Colin could just see the fresh grave and Minister Fairchild delivering a eulogy to a large group of people dressed in black.

Sam Bale's funeral.

The funeral was coming to an end. Colin caught the smell of fresh roses and watched as the attendees dropped the flowers into the grave, saying their final good-byes.

Colin wanted to pay his respects but, following Silas' advice, decided to wait until everyone had cleared out. A familiar stench hit him, and Colin looked over to see the bulky frame of Gareth Dugan hiding behind a large angel statue. It was the same smell from the other night. Gareth's personal odor wasn't like other humans. There were also traces of sadness there, and a lot of anger. Anger smelled like burned food. It was distasteful and almost made Colin want to throw up. Colin made a mental note to write down the different smells associated with each emotion. Gareth saw Colin watching him and walked over.

Oh, great. This is all I need.

As Gareth got closer, Colin noticed something else about the bully who normally made his life miserable. His eyes were red and glassy, like he'd been crying. Was he crying because he was guilty, hurt, or sad?

Colin's mind whirled as he searched for answers.

"Hi, Colin," said Gareth.

"Gareth," nodded Colin politely.

"Listen, sorry about the other night. I was angry and upset and ..."

Gareth trailed off, and Colin was too stunned at the apology to say anything.

"Anyway, did you and Becca get away okay?"

Colin blinked a few times and worked to make his mouth move.

"Uh, yeah. We did. You too? Well of course, you're here. And the cops didn't mention anything."

"Yeah, they came to visit me too. Angered my dad something rotten."

Is he sharing with me? Is this a bonding moment?

"Well, don't think this makes us friends or anything," assured Gareth. But there was no punch behind it, no sneer. Colin actually smiled.

"Of course not. Wouldn't dream of it."

Gareth turned and walked away.

Was Gareth Dugan the other werewolf? Had he killed one of his friends and now the guilt was tearing him apart? Or was Colin looking too hard for a suspect other than himself?

Colin shook the feeling off; it wasn't a road he wanted to go down right now. Heading to the now-empty gravesite, Colin closed his eyes, allowing his senses to open as he sniffed the air and listened to his surroundings. The cemetery workers would soon come to fill in the grave, but for now it was just Colin and the corpse.

In his mind, he could picture the world around him

in vibrant colors. The same way he had at the crime scene, and then again in the basement at the Baker farm. The fragrance from the roses on the grave were overpoweringly strong, as was the polish on the coffin. The dirt was damp; he could hear people in the parking lot leaving. Concentrating hard, he could pinpoint individuals. Perfume. Bad breath. Cigarette smoke. Chinese food. Sweat. So many different smells defining different people.

Something however was missing. Focusing on the grave, he breathed in heavily through his nose. Roses. Polish. Wood. Dirt. Cloth. Water. Nothing else. He couldn't smell the body. Colin opened his eyes and looked around. There was the faint silhouette of Gareth, but he was a long way away, past the edge of the cemetery. Colin looked toward the cemetery entrance to see the last car leaving the parking lot.

What am I thinking? I can't! But I have to know!

Colin took a last glance around and dropped into the grave, landing on top of the coffin. He put his legs to either side and pulled open the coffin lid.

Empty!

The body of Sam Bale was missing.

Chapter Eleven

Growing Pains

Later that night, Colin sat in his room with a notepad and wrote down everything that had happened to him. As he did so, he realized his thought process was also improving. He was an average student and never really excelled at anything, but since being bitten, he found he could think faster, or maybe just clearer, as his earlier conversation with Becca had shown.

So far, he'd filled ten pages with messy notes detailing what he remembered of getting bitten and that first night. Next came the timeline of events. The first time his senses had emerged. His hair growth. When his muscles started to appear. The hallucinations, the blackouts, the dreams. He noticed there was a real wave effect to everything. Painful changes would occur followed by a noticeable, increased strength in that area. He detailed the meaning of different smells. Recalling the biology lesson on pheromones, Colin concluded that it wasn't just odors he smelled but also pheromones! That would explain why he could read emotions.

The most painful part was lining his timeline of events up with the murder of Sam Bale. There was absolutely no way he could recall where he had been when Sam was killed. If Silas was correct, then he had been in full-on wolf mode, his body reacting to the initial bite. All he clearly remembered was stalking, killing, and eating a deer.

Colin's stomach lurched but not in a sick-sort of way. He was hungry again. After he'd found Sam's coffin to be empty, he'd continued with his original plan and stopped by the store to get shaving supplies. On impulse, he bought two full bags of snack food. So far he'd consumed all the chips, granola bars, and beef jerky. The thought of eating that deer sickened him but also made him drool a little.

Shake it off, Colin! Where am I going to find a deer at this time of night? It's not like I can order take-out.

He'd also started making a list of suspects. Sadly, his own name was at the top. Other suspects included the mystery floating man from the alley, Silas Baxter, Gareth Dugan, Mr. Emerson, and any one of the black-suited people intent on capturing Silas. Not knowing where else to start, he decided he would ask Becca about her father tomorrow at school. He didn't want to push her for information, but he had to know. There was a killer on the loose, and he had to figure out who it was. Even if it turned out to be himself.

Before bed, Colin shaved for the first time in his

entire life. It took him an hour. Partially because he'd never done it before and partially because the hair was so thick. He suspected he'd have to shave again in the morning and had already planned to wear baggy clothing to help cover his new physique.

Colin stripped down to his underwear and began sniffing everything in his room to ensure he got a good night sleep. Not even attempting to sleep like a normal person, he just curled into a ball on top of his covers and drifted off. He thought he could faintly hear Silas's voice, but Colin was too tired to acknowledge it.

Sleep well, wolf-pup.

***

The alarm didn't even get a chance to go off at 6:00 a.m. Colin's stomach had already woken him up at 5:30 a.m. demanding to be fed. He had quietly slipped downstairs, defrosted a steak, and eaten the whole thing without cooking it. Two bowls of cornflakes, a glass of juice, and six pieces of toast later, and Colin finally felt full. He made his way to the bathroom, stopping as he caught his reflection. "Hair," said Colin, which proved to be a bit of an understatement.

His dark hair was no longer straggly; it was fuller, richer, like he'd stepped out of a high-priced shampoo commercial. The beard he had shaved the night before had already grown back. It was short, but a beard nonetheless. His forearms, legs, and chest were now showing signs of hair growth, but that wasn't nearly as impressive as his muscle development. Colin bordered on skeletal just a few days ago. Now he could pass for an athlete. The muscles weren't bulky, but they were defined.

I have a six-pack!

With everything going on, Colin knew that he shouldn't feel any joy at all in what was happening. He might be a murderer. But—

I look amazing!

As an unwanted, unloved teenager with the skin complexion of a hobo and the body mass of an under-fed stick insect, it was impossible for Colin not to find joy in this change.

Colin shaved, showered, and then dressed in the baggiest clothing he owned. He packed his notepad and—

Bacon!

The enticing aroma of cooking bacon hit him, and his stomach suddenly felt less full. Leaping from the top of the stairs and landing lightly at the bottom, Colin was in the kitchen before he'd even decided to leave his bedroom.

His grandmother was frying a pan of bacon, and the smell was intoxicating. A year ago, Colin would have been trying to figure out how a blind old lady was able to cook, but he'd since stopped worrying about it and accepted that his grandmother was more than able to do things. Blind or not.

"What do you want?" asked his grandmother.

"Could I have some of that?" said Colin, his mouth watering.

"Over a year you've lived here and you've never asked

me to make you breakfast," stated his grandmother. She didn't sound angry, she sounded more surprised.

"I always assumed you wouldn't want to."

She let out a sharp laugh. "Well this is just a week for surprises, isn't it?"

Colin gratefully accepted a plate piled high with over half the bacon from the pan. He sat at the small table and started to devour it. "Thank you," said Colin between bites.

The old woman plated her own food and sat across from Colin. "Something's happened to you, boy."

Silas's advice of keeping a low profile rang through his head. Interacting with his grandmother was definitely out of the ordinary. "Probably just, uh, a growth spurt?"

His grandmother's eyes narrowed. "Not just the food, there's something else. This gallivanting around at night with strange girls. Watch out for that Emerson girl, she can raise hell!"

"I ... it's ... well—"

"Can it! Over a year you've been here. Barely any friends, nothing special about you at all, and all of a sudden you're eating like a horse, talking back to me, and hanging out with a girl. And you look different too!"

"Grandma, you're blind."

"Not so blind that I don't see what's going on in my own town. You mark my words, boy! You be careful. Elkwood is a fragile town. We all do our part. You be careful you don't break it."

"I have to go." Colin left the table and headed down the hallway.

"Colin," said his grandmother, "I'll be watching you."

Colin headed out the front door.

Well that was creepy and uncomfortable.

The fog was thick as Colin started his trek to school. He was tempted to run, to feel the wind in his face; he could be at school in less than five minutes. But the conversation with his grandmother had shaken him and running at inhuman speeds through town, even with the fog, would likely raise suspicion. Colin couldn't figure out whether his grandmother knew something or if she was just essentially unsettling. Maybe it was both?

Colin walked past the cemetery on his way to school and saw that Sam's empty casket was now buried.

Colin passed kind, old Mrs. Flipple walking her yappy dog, Jinx, who took one look at Colin and bolted, ripping the leash out of Mrs. Flipple's hands.

"Yipe! yipe! yipe! yipe!" was all that could be heard from Jinx as he vanished into the fog followed by a shuffling Mrs. Flipple.

"Come back here, Jinxy! What's gotten into you?" called Mrs. Flipple.

Colin smiled.

Yappy mutt.

When Colin arrived, the imposing figure of Principal Hebert guarded the school steps as usual. The schoolyard was busy this morning as students gathered, whispering about Sam Bale's mysterious death. Colin's ears picked up everything.

"I heard that it was a mountain lion."

"—human sacrifice—"

"—drug problem—"

"Gareth Dugan killed him over a candy bar."

"—people visited the crime scene."

"Principal Hebert did it because Sam never turned his homework in on time."

"—a genetically altered goat, bred by the government as a covert killing machine got loose and—"

"The police came to my house on Saturday."

"—hear a gunshot on Friday?"

"Do you think it'll happen again?

"Who will be next?"

"Mr. Strauss," boomed the deep baritone voice of Principal Hebert.

Colin found himself standing in front of the imposing figure. "Oh, hello, Principal Hebert."

"It's nice to see you on time for once."

"Yes, I made a special effort this morning."

My stomach alarm went off.

"Let's try to make it a habit, shall we?"

"I'll work on that, sir."

"See that you do."

Colin entered the school and grabbed some books from his locker, immediately picking up two familiar scents. One made his heart skip a beat, the other made him feel a little ill. Down the hallway, Becca was opening her locker when Gareth Dugan approached her. Even with all the kids in the hallway, Colin could pick up their voices clearly.

"Becca," said Gareth.

"Hi, Gareth. How are you feeling?"

Colin watched as Gareth rubbed his shoulder.

"It feels cold sometimes, but otherwise I'm fine."

"That'll happen for a while. You're lucky it wasn't worse."

"Yeah, well. I just wanted to … uh … say, um, thanks. I don't fully remember everything but I … well, thanks."

Becca smiled politely as Gareth turned and walked away.

What was that about?

The first period bell rang, and Colin felt like someone was trying to pull his brain out through his ears. He crouched down and covered his ears until the ringing stopped. When he stood up, Becca was next to him, concern painted across her face. She smelled good.

"Hi, Colin, you okay?"

"Becca, hey. Yeah, just a headache."

"What did you do to your hair?"

Colin's hoodie had slipped off. He must look strange. "Oh, that. It's a, uh, new shampoo. Natural ingredients adds a, uh, lustrous shine."

Becca smiled. "It looks good. Suits you. Come on. Winter will have our heads if we're late."

Ugh, Monday morning biology. As if turning into a hairy killing machine wasn't enough!

As they walked into class, Colin's nose was hit with an overwhelming blast of strong aftershave. Like someone had bathed in it.

"Take your seats, take your seats!" barked Mr. Winter.

Colin could practically see vapors rising off Mr. Winter. He was the one wearing the aftershave. A gallon of it. It made Colin's head swim. Had he always worn so much? It was highly likely and Colin had just never noticed before. Now, thanks to his super sense of smell, it was impossible to ignore. It was like being slapped in the nostrils over and over again.

Colin and Becca took their usual seats. Jeremy looking as spritely as ever.

"Hey, Col. How was the weekend? Did you hear that someone went out to the crime scene?"

"Oh yeah? Was that you?"

Jeremy looked disappointed. "No, couldn't convince anyone to go with me. But apparently there was a gunshot out there on Friday night."

"I heard something about that. But you know me, stayed home all weekend."

"What do you think of Winter's new do?"

"What?"

Looking at Mr. Winter, Colin realized the grumpy old teacher had shaved his head.

"He's gone full militant!" said Jeremy, stifling a laugh.

Wondering what else he hadn't noticed, Colin looked around the class.

Gareth and Kevin were in their same old spots, but they both looked tired, and Colin could smell their depression.

Nothing like one of your friends being killed to take the fun out of bullying people.

The goth twins were absent.

Tori wasn't here yet either, but she was often late. When you're gorgeous, you can get away with pretty much anything.

"Principal Hebert," said Mr. Winter, "has asked me to remind you all that a grief counselor will be available all this week if anyone wants to talk about the unfortunate passing of our friend Mr. Bale. I for one will miss Mr. Bale's inability to hand in even one piece of homework on time."

"Did he just make a joke about the violent death of a student?" whispered Jeremy.

"Apparently," said Colin.

"Do you two have something to add? Mr. Strauss? Mr. Rodson? No, nothing. Then shut up!"

Mr. Winter started droning on about gray matter and the lack of brain functionality in his class, but Colin found it hard to concentrate. The aftershave was giving him a headache.

Without warning, an intoxicating fire washed over him, threatening to consume his entire body. Starting to sweat and breathing heavily, he tried to focus, but his senses were going haywire.

"Sorry I'm late," said Tori, walking in.

"Ms. Clemens, so nice of you to grace us with your presence," said Mr. Winter.

Whatever was setting Colin off was coming from Tori. She was the most beautiful, awe-inspiring thing he had ever encountered in his life, literally emanating some kind of force. He wanted nothing more than to kiss her.

Colin gripped his desk, panting.

"You all right?" asked Jeremy. "You're looking a bit weird."

Mr. Winter thundered over. "Really, Mr. Strauss? Another episode? Do you have some sort of allergy to biology?"

What is happening to me now?

Colin, what's going on?

Silas! I don't know, I'm sweating and breathing heavy and ...

And what?

Colin tried to think of the best way to phrase what he was currently feeling.

I love her; I want to kiss her. I really, really want to kiss her.

For a moment, he thought he could hear Silas laughing inside his head.

I want her! I must have her!

Who's her?

Tori! Tori Clemens. Hottest girl in school. In the world!

Colin, this shouldn't be happening. You'll get these emotional urges, and they'll be stronger because you're part animal, but nothing like this. Describe what you're feeling.

I feel like I'm on fire. I can hear everything. I can smell everyone. Everything. I can't see straight. And my heart's going to explode.

Colin doubled over in pain.

"Mr. Rodson, be so kind as to take Mr. Strauss to the nurse."

"I'll take him," said Becca quickly, not waiting for a response. She grabbed Colin's arm and helped him off his stool, but Colin could barely move.

Colin, this is important. What's your skin feel like?

It feels tingly, like its moving!

Colin, listen carefully, you're changing. Strong sensations, violent acts, powerful emotions. If you can't control them, they'll cause a change. You're young. You can't control it yet. You have to get out of there.

Colin turned his head to look at Tori who had taken her seat. Her hair was curly today, she was wearing a tight

• 117 •

shirt that accented her ample bosom, and her skirt was so short that the word *mini* didn't do it justice. She perched on the stool like a beautiful Greek statue.

"Colin," urged Becca in a whisper, "you have to move. Your eyes are doing that weird thing again. They look brighter."

Becca says my eyes are changing color.

Colin! You have to get out of there now! Whatever this girl Tori is, she's not supposed to have this effect on you. She might not even be human!

What?

Get out now!

Mr. Winter was furiously shouting for order as Becca tried to unsuccessfully move a panting Colin as the entire class watched, laughing. Looking down, Colin saw that one of his nails had grown long and curled itself into a claw. He quickly shoved the hand in his pocket and surrendered control to Becca to get him out of the classroom.

"Air!" gasped Colin as they staggered into the hallway. They moved quickly toward the nearest exit and out into the cool misty air.

"What's happening to you, Colin? You're burning up!" demanded Becca as they made their way toward the empty football field.

"Tori." was all Colin could say.

"Tori?" Becca repeated, a wave of jealousy wafting from her.

Had Colin not felt like he was dying he would have been flattered.

"Not. Like. That."

His jaw hurt. It felt like his teeth were growing inside his mouth. His limbs felt heavy, like they were expanding.

Colin, you have to get away. You're too far along and you're too young. You won't be able to stop the change. Run, now! Head for the forest to the east of the school. I'll find you!

Colin pulled away from Becca, and despite his skin feeling like it was trying to melt off his body, he started running across the football field toward the forest.

"Colin!" shouted Becca.

"Later!" said Colin, picking up speed.

You're not due for a change until the next full moon. This is going to hurt. A lot. Listen to me, listen to my voice!

Colin barely heard a word. He plunged through the thicket of trees, running for what seemed like an eternity until he couldn't fight the pain anymore and collapsed next to a creek running through the forest. Slurping greedily at the water with cupped hands, Colin realized his hands weren't normal. They were bigger, and each finger was tipped with a black claw that looked like it could tear through metal. Silas continued to drone on in his head, but he couldn't catch any distinct words.

I'm turning! I'm turning into a werewolf!

He felt scared, excited, powerful, and nervous all at once. Colin pulled off his hoodie and tried to get his jeans undone, which proved difficult with claws. He kicked off his shoes and lay on the ground gulping air, wearing only underwear and a T-shirt.

Maybe I'm not changing. Maybe it's going away.

That's when the pain really started.

Chapter Twelve

The First Turn

The change tore through him like a dump truck barrelling through a glass factory. It felt like the worst muscle cramp in the world multiplied by a hundred, covered in gasoline, and then set on fire. Colin's heart pumped the change throughout his body, every beat bringing new pain, a new sensation. His body convulsed and heaved as his skin stretched to accommodate his expanding muscles. Colin writhed on the ground, feeling his bones lengthen under his skin. His legs grew and stretched into the hind leg of a canine; his feet shifted into a massive paw tipped with vicious claws.

Colin's jaw and nose grew into a snout, his teeth sharpening in his mouth, ears extending toward the top of his head. His vision blurred as his eyes enlarged and then everything snapped into a blindingly, perfect clarity. Flailing on the ground and gasping for breath, he heard his voice change, becoming guttural, animalistic. He was growling!

His arms, legs, chest, stomach, hips, back all made the most disgusting clicking sounds as his bones realigned, muscles expanding around them. Underwear and shirt ripping as his body exploded in size, Colin could tell he was bigger; he even felt heavier. Last of all, hair erupted over his body. One minute skin, the next, hair. Everywhere! It grew fast and thick, covering his entire body. A final wave of pain ran through him, and then Colin stood on all fours and let out a long howl that resonated around the forest.

He heard Silas before he saw him, but it wasn't the same man from before. This was Silas, the creature. Leaping from the trees, he landed lightly on his hind legs in front of Colin.

Can you hear me, Colin?

I'm ... I'm not me.

You are you! You're just a different you.

Do I look like you?

See for yourself.

Silas pointed toward the creek with one massive, clawed finger.

Colin turned, still on all fours and walked shakily toward the creek. Everything around him was clear and bright. With each inhalation, his focus improved. Looking down into the still water, Colin saw himself for the first time.

He was hideous and beautiful. His fur was a deep charcoal gray, and his eyes like bright amber. His head was shaped like a wolf's, but it much bigger. Like Silas, he had grown an extra three to four feet, his body proportionate to his new height. Pawing at the water, he discovered his hands were still hands only they were much bigger, covered in hair, and each finger was tipped with a vicious-looking claw.

Pushing himself to his feet, or rather, his back paws, Colin stretched to his full height.

You can run on two legs or four. You'll find there are advantages to both.

I'm a monster.

Colin thought it, but he didn't truly feel that way. Truthfully, he felt amazing.

Never feel guilty for what you are! This is a gift, Colin. If you use it and learn to control it, it can be something magnificent. If you abuse it, you'll destroy yourself.

Why was my change different?

It could be because I'm older than most, or maybe your genetic make-up is more accepting of the wolf gene. Or it could be this place. It could be Elkwood.

Colin turned, almost losing his balance but regaining it almost instantly.

Why do I feel so shaky?

You're a lot bigger than you're used to. It won't take long for your body to right itself. Your instincts will sharpen the more you move around.

Why did I change just now? What happened to me back there, and if Tori aren't human, then what is she?

Silas dropped to all fours, sitting down on his haunches.

Well isn't that just the question of the day? Your

change can be triggered by strong emotions: anger, hate, jealousy, fear ... a sense of love in this case.

I don't love Tori, but that feeling was so strong. At that moment, I felt like I did love her, like I couldn't live without her! What is she?

I don't know what she is. But I have an idea of how you can find out.

Me? Why me? Why not you? You're the werewolf-hunting werewolf!

I told you. They're tracking me.

The mystery men in the black suits?

Silas nodded.

Can we talk normally while in this form?

"We can." Silas's voice was a low growl, and he spoke slowly, carefully forming the words. "But it takes practice." **Much easier to just project your thoughts. You can even speak to some humans this way, but they have to have an open mind to hear your thoughts.**

I'm just a teenager, Silas. I'm not ready for any of this.

Too late now. Had I known for certain that I was going to live that night, I never would have bitten you. But I didn't know. I was scared.

Colin laughed, but it came out as a sort of *bark.*

It's not funny. After living as long as I have, death is one of the few things left to actually fear.

Colin measured the creature sitting before him. Silas looked beyond powerful and imposing. Colin's head swam with questions. He decided to shoot for the most obvious.

How strong am I?

It depends. You've already noticed how strong you

are as a human. Your strength is doubled in your wolf form.

So I'm not immortal?

No, you can definitely die.

Colin was a little disappointed. He was hoping for a *live-forever* sort of deal.

You will live a longer life than any human. The oldest werewolf I've ever met was almost 800 years old, but he didn't look so good.

Am I bulletproof?

Silas gave a throaty growl that Colin realized was actually a laugh.

Not exactly. Bullets won't bounce off you. They'll hurt horribly, but your body will regenerate quickly.

Like Wolverine!

I don't know who that is. You can heal from almost any injury whether you're in human or wolf form. There are certain things that will kill you. If your head gets cut off, it's pretty much game over. You can't regenerate from that. If another werewolf eats your heart, you're done.

Lots of rules. I feel like a Gremlin.

Don't know what that is either.

It's a movie. Have you been living under a rock?

Sometimes. Silver is the other thing you need to be aware of.

Silver bullets? That's actually a thing?

Silver of any kind will irritate your skin. If you're wounded from a silver bullet or cut with a silver blade, you'll heal at a normal human rate. If you lose too much blood from a wound like that, you can definitely die.

Got it. So definitely not immortal?

Nope. You do look bigger than I do though.

How's that even possible?

The change affects everyone differently. You're going to be a strong werewolf, Colin.

You said I could find out what Tori is? How do I do it?

Go to a town hall meeting. I think it'll prove to be a real eye-opener. There's one tonight.

Impossible, they only have them once a month.

I overheard there is going to be another one tonight. Apparently, the last one ended early. Probably because I came to town.

You know more than you're letting on.

I have theories. I can't prove anything, and I think you need to learn a few things for yourself. Who knows? Maybe you'll be able to make more sense out of all this.

And the other werewolf?

He's still in town.

I could still be the killer, couldn't I?

You could be. We don't know for sure. This other werewolf is a known killer. That's why I'm tracking him. Could you have killed that boy? Absolutely. But it's also more than possible it was the other werewolf in town.

How do I know you're not the killer?

Look into my mind, kid. You can see everything. I can't see your first night as a werewolf because you weren't even conscious yourself. We're connected right now, concentrate on this connection. Take a peek. Did I kill him?

Colin tilted his head like a confused dog. He concentrated on Silas's mind. There was death there; the events all strung together like a badly edited movie. Centuries of hunting and killing crammed into a single shot of memory. Sam Bale wasn't in there.

It wasn't you.

I'll keep hunting the other werewolf. You head to that meeting tonight and see if you can find out what's going on. You'll need to change back. Whoever these men in suits are, they seem to be able to track me when I'm in wolf form. No point in you showing up on their radar.

With that, Silas leaped high into the sky, grabbing hold of a tree with his powerful claws. He continued jumping, climbing higher and higher into the dense forest until he was lost from sight. Colin could still faintly hear his thoughts and thought of one last question.

Wait, how do I change back?

Imagine yourself as a human.

It's that simple?

It's that simple.

Will it hurt?

It'll always hurt. Although it won't be like this first time. Your body remembers. The change will become faster. Good luck, Colin. If you need me, think loud thoughts.

With that last bit of advice, Silas slipped smoothly out of his head, and Colin was alone again.

Preparing to jump, Colin crouched and sprang into the air, at least twenty feet, landing lightly next to the creek. He wanted find out what he was capable of.

Silas's warning about the black suits' ability to track his movements as a wolf rang in his head, and he knew he should turn back.

But he didn't want to. Not yet.

I'm a werewolf. I'm a freakin' werewolf!

Colin took off at a run, first on two legs, then dropping to all four. Four legs were better for speed, but two gave him better manoeuvrability. He bounded high into the trees and climbed the large trunks, his claws digging easily into the wood.

Vaulting from tree to tree like a monkey, he dropped back to the ground, his claws digging into the dirt as he ran. As his senses absorbed the various sounds and smells of the woods, a familiar something tingled down his spine.

Becca.

He could hear her searching for him at least a mile away. Calling his name. There was no way he could let her see him like this. As much as the thought pained him, he had to change back. Colin returned to the creek to retrieve his clothes.

He flexed his senses, extending his awareness, one last time before attempting the change.

I could get used to this.

Chapter Thirteen

Conversations

Changing back was just as painful but took less time. As soon as Colin decided to change, the hair instantly shed from his body like someone shaking a pine tree, falling away and disintegrating into nothingness. At the same time, his body contorted and twisted rapidly. Colin imagined it looked like someone unfolding an origami swan, or wolf in this case, and refolding it into a boy.

Bones shrank, disconnecting, and reconnecting in a string of sickening clicks and crunches. Muscles burning as they deflated back down to size. The beautiful claws at the tips of his fingers and toes shrank and uncurled into regular human nails. His skin, which was now much too big for his body, shrink-wrapped around his newly reformed bones and muscles while a faint tingle signalled the regrowth of his human body hair.

The whole thing took only a few seconds. He stood naked in the forest by the creek. In human form, he had super-human strength and senses but as a wolf, everything was magnified so much more. He still didn't know if he was a killer, but if this was his life now, then Colin was determined to be the best werewolf there was. He wasn't going to squander these gifts and momentarily pictured himself in spandex and fighting crime.

Ridiculous. I'd look horrible in spandex.

Looking at his reflection in the water as he pulled his jeans back on, Colin felt as if the change had balanced everything out. He had abs and unmistakable muscle definition while his eyes shined with an amber tinge and his hair was thick and messy.

The body of a monster. This is so cool.

"Colin?" Becca's voice was full of disbelief, shock, confusion, embarrassment ... lots of embarrassment.

Spinning around, Colin found Becca standing at the edge of the tree line, her mouth frozen open. Colin had been so wrapped up in his thoughts he'd been ignoring his new senses that he was currently obsessing over.

"I ... Becca ...," stammered Colin, scrambling for a plausible reason as to why he was standing half-naked next to a creek in the middle of a forest. He needed something creative, something amazing, something that would cause no room for argument.

"I was really warm," he finally managed. "So I was going to cool myself off in the creek."

"Colin, you're hot." She suddenly realized that she was staring and covered her own eyes. "I mean, you're hot? You were hot. Like a fever. That's why ... yes, that explains it. Wow. Okay. I'm just going to …" She turned to face the other way. "Maybe you should finish getting dressed"

Huh? She's just as flustered as me.

Colin grabbed his discarded hoodie, pulling it over his head. "I'm really sorry, Becca. I didn't feel well, I couldn't catch my breath, and then I found myself here and, well, I feel better now."

"Please tell me you're fully clothed."

Colin slipped his sneakers back on his feet. He picked up the T-shirt and underwear he'd torn to shreds when he changed, balled them, and threw them into some bushes, making a mental note to buy some stretchy clothing.

"Okay, I'm good. I mean, I'm dressed. I … yeah, this is awkward."

Becca turned around, a smile playing at the corners of her mouth. "I was worried when you ran off like that, so I came looking for you after class ended. That was a little more of you than I was expecting to find."

Walking back through the forest, Colin asked Becca. "Did I miss anything good in class?"

"Mr. Winter was furious with you. I thought he was going to blow a gasket. He was so worked up that he dismissed class early."

"That man has some serious anger issues."

"Can you believe he made another joke about Sam's death? That's really weird, right?"

"He does seem to be a bigger jerk lately. And that aftershave!"

"What does he do? Bathe in the stuff? Are you feeling better?"

Her hand felt cold against his forehead as she checked for a fever. The lurching of his insides having nothing to do with the crushing feelings he felt for her. It felt like somebody was poking around inside his body, exploring his mind. Looking at Becca, he could see her eyes moving beneath her closed lids.

Colin stepped away, and her eyes snapped open. She looked confused for a second.

"What are you doing?" said Colin.

"I was checking to see if you still had a fever. You have to admit you've been acting strange lately."

There was a waver in her voice, and her heartbeat had noticeably increased a few clicks. *She's lying.*

They walked on in silence. Colin thought back to the day Gareth and his cronies had beaten him in detention, when Becca had pulled him aside and he'd gotten that same sensation. Something wasn't right. And it wasn't just Becca or Tori or the man in the alley or the wolf attack. It was Elkwood; something wasn't right with Elkwood.

They reached the football field in time to hear the bell ring for lunch.

"I think I'm going to head home early," said Colin.

"Are you okay? Maybe you should see a doctor."

The only doctor in town was Dr. Flint, and he was a notorious drunk who was just as likely to fall asleep during an appointment, as he was to diagnose the common cold as Ebola.

"I'll think about it. Talk later?"

"Yeah. I'll call you."

Colin turned and left her standing there. Until recently, he was a quiet loser with no aspirations. Now *this* had happened, and he felt like he was seeing the world for the first time. His normal *modus operandi* would be to ignore everything content to let the world pass him by. Now he felt a nagging need to know what was going on and why. Curiosity often killed the cat, but for the first time in his life, Colin didn't care.

If curiosity tries to kill me, I'll bite its head off.

***

It was raining heavily by the time Colin got home. He briefly considered slipping around the back of the house and jumping to the roof to climb in his bedroom window. But he'd learned long ago that sneaking past his grandmother was impossible; she had ears like a bat. Instead, he told her he wasn't feeling well and ran up the stairs before she had a chance to respond. She muttered several curse words which, thanks to his newfound hearing abilities, Colin heard from his bedroom.

He spent the rest of the afternoon writing out everything he could remember about his first change, even the minor details. Four hours later, he'd filled another notepad. With the memories still fresh in his mind, he considered trying to change again; in truth, he was craving it. He had a strong desire to assume his wolf form again, to experience the thrill of running through the forest, hunting deer … His stomach growled as his nose caught the whiff of Bolognese sauce.

"Dinner's ready!" shouted his grandmother.

She made me dinner?

Colin wasn't in any hurry to repeat this morning's awkward exchange with his grandmother, but the smell of food was difficult to resist. Before he'd really thought about it, he was already downstairs standing in the kitchen. His grandmother was straining pasta over the sink.

"Since you've acquired the appetite of a horse, I thought I'd make us dinner," said his grandmother.

"I don't really know what to say." And he truly didn't. This was all too unusual.

"You can start with a thank-you. I'm nobody's slave."

"Thank you."

"Now be a good useless teenager and dish up food."

His grandmother removed her apron and took her usual seat at the kitchen table. Colin loaded two plates with pasta and meat sauce and sat down across from the old lady who had terrified him for the past year. It was like sitting down with an old enemy to discuss a ceasefire. Maybe that's exactly what this was.

"Feeling better?" asked his grandmother.

"Yes, thank you, Grandmother."

They both ate in silence. Colin finished off one plate of food and went for a second.

"I'm going to a town hall meeting tonight at seven o'clock. I expect it'll run late," she informed him.

Silas was right.

"Didn't you just have a town hall meeting?"

"We didn't finish discussing all the issues at the last one."

Colin wondered how far he should or could push for

information. "What happens at these meetings?"

"Nothing of great interest. We'll discuss different issues and possible developments for the town. What will you be doing tonight? More gallivanting through the night with your strange new friends?"

Colin ignored the not-so-subtle poke. "I think I'll head to bed early. I want to rest up in case I am getting sick."

"Hmph. For a sick kid, you've got a healthy appetite."

Colin finished off his second plate and loaded the dishes into the dishwasher. He grabbed a couple slices of garlic bread, thanked his grandmother for dinner, and headed upstairs.

At 6:15 p.m., his cell phone buzzed.

"Hello?" answered Colin.

"Hi, Colin. How are you feeling?" It was Becca.

"I think I'm okay. How was the rest of school?"

"Oh, it was the same exceptionally amazing educational experience that it always is. Jeremy seemed worried about you."

"No he didn't. Jeremy never worries about anything."

"Yeah, you're right. He didn't. Does he always strike you as being blissfully unaware?"

"I'd say that sums up Jer perfectly."

"Good-looking guy though."

Wait, what?

"I …well, if you like those sorts of boyish good looks, I suppose so."

"Do you know if he's seeing anyone?"

Jealousy gripped Colin like a vise, and he felt the creature inside him begin to move. He remembered Silas's words: *"Your change can be triggered by strong emotions."*

"No," said Colin through gritted teeth, "he's not seeing anyone."

Suddenly Becca laughed. Colin loved her laugh. Skin tingling and sweating profusely, Colin fought to control his body.

Heart racing, he glanced in the mirror, understanding what Becca had meant before about his eyes. They were a bright golden amber color.

"I'm just screwing with you, Colin!" said Becca amid her laughter. "I have no interest in Jeremy."

The tingling vanished, Colin's heart slowed, and he watched as his eyes dimmed but that new amber tint remained. He took a deep breath. "Yeah, I knew that."

Subject change, need a subject change.

"So what's on the agenda tonight?" said Colin. "More midnight crime scene investigations, or are you going to go full-on rebellious and start digging up graves?"

"Is that what full rebel is? Had I only known. I've been a full rebel for years."

"You have a real creepy side to you, you know that?"

"Well, Colin, we all have secrets, don't we?"

"Do we?"

There was an uncomfortable pause. Colin could hear Becca breathing. He toyed with the idea of telling her about Sam Bale's body not being in the casket, but since their encounter in the woods, he just didn't feel comfortable revealing something that big. Not yet at least.

"I'm probably just going to turn in early," admitted Becca. "You should probably do the same. Running around half-naked in the woods can't be good for your health."

"I wouldn't say that. It's quite invigorating. You should try it."

"Oh, no thank you, Mr. Strauss. I'll leave that to the professionals."

"I'm hardly a professional. Semi-professional at best."

Becca laughed. He heard the front door open and close downstairs as his grandmother left for the town hall meeting.

"Have a good night, Becca. Sweet dreams."

"Hey, Colin?"

"Yes?"

"As much fun as the crime scene thing was, do you think, I mean —"

Colin heard her heart speed up.

She's nervous.

"—what I'm trying to say," said Becca, "would you be interested in just hanging out one night? Normally?"

Colin didn't miss a beat. "I'd love that! Yes, absolutely!"

"Okay, great."

There was relief in her voice. She had been nervous!

A girl asked me out, and she was nervous about it!

If Colin had kept a diary, this definitely would have gone in there. He was almost tempted to add it to his werewolf notebook.

"Good night, Colin," said Becca. "I'll try not to show up in your room tonight."

"Only in my dreams."

Oh God, that was cheesy. Why did I say that? Why? Why? Why? Why? Why?—

Becca laughed. "You're cute. G'night, Colin."

Phew.

Chapter Fourteen

Town Hall Chaos

Fog had already settled across the town when Colin, dressed in dark clothing, exited the house and made his way downtown. Hoping not to get caught, he had given his grandmother ample time to make it to the town hall. Colin felt he was practically becoming an expert at sneaking around at night. He could easily add it to his list of *special skills*.

Sure, right next to my other special skill. I can turn into a large wolf creature with superhuman strength and speed and can smell a fart from literally a block away.

Built by the founding fathers of Elkwood, the town hall was a stately old building situated on the outskirts of downtown Colin had only seen the interior once when his grandmother had dragged him to the annual craft fair. He remembered it to be a large hall with hardwood floors and an interior balcony that stretched around the perimeter. There were only two entrances to the building. The double doors in the front were the main entrance, but there was no way Colin would get in that way without being noticed. There was also a back door that led to a small kitchen, but Colin was thinking of something a little more creative.

To be honest, Colin was dying to try out some rooftop escapades. If he could jump great distances, then why not travel across the roofs of the downtown buildings and climb in through one of the second-story balcony windows?

Downtown was deserted, much like the night he'd stolen his grandfather's car. The only sound of activity came directly from the town hall two streets over.

Colin gave a final glance around and easily jumped from the ground to the roof of the convenience store. He landed lightly on the edge, gauging the distance from his current position to the roof of the old movie theater. He ran a few steps, panicked, and skidded to a stop, almost falling off the building.

Come on. It's just a few, ten … thirty feet.

Just this morning, he'd leaped from tree to tree as a giant wolf. A short jump across the street should be nothing.

Colin shook off his nerves and returned to the far edge of the rooftop. He took a deep breath and started running, very conscious of his muscles, muscles he hadn't had a few days ago. He leaped, momentum and sheer force of will propelling him across the wide gap, and landed on the opposing roof with ease.

This. Is. Amazing!

Many recognizable and new smells floated to Colin as he crept slowly to the roof's edge and peaked over. The fog was less dense around the building, and Colin could easily see the town hall standing quietly, windows brightly lit. Unusual, however, were the two armed guards wearing dark suits and earpieces standing outside the open front doors.

Who are these guys?

Colin could clearly hear the buzz of voices inside. A shadow loomed across the front porch of the town hall and the imposing figure of Mr. Emerson exited the building and spoke to the guard on the left. Colin listened intently, easily picking up their conversation even at this distance.

"Is everything secure, Agent Drake?" asked Mr. Emerson.

"Affirmative, sir," replied Drake. "Alpha team will arrive soon and sweep the grid. Nothing will get in or out tonight."

"See that it doesn't. We have two confirmed predators loose in the town, and the stooges have determined a possible third."

Stooges?

"Three of them, sir?"

"Maybe they're breeding?" suggested the other guard.

Mr. Emerson shook his head and returned to the building, closing the doors behind him. Colin heard the distinct click of the door locking.

"Maybe they're breeding?" said Drake sarcastically. "Seriously?"

"What?" said the other guard with a shrug. "We

started out with one last week, then a second, and now a possible third. What's your explanation?"

"We know practically nothing about these things. You'd think after everything we've seen we'd have come across one somewhere. Who knows how they multiply."

"They're breeding."

"You're an idiot."

Colin could hear a truck approaching.

Must be the Alpha team. Time to move.

Skin tingling, Colin wanted so badly to change, to feel the comfort of growing into the wolf creature, to feel his senses soar. It was like a drug. A strange, powerful, hairy drug. With teeth.

Keeping low, he crept to the back of the building and dropped down into the back alley. He followed the length of the block and doubled back, quickly crossing the main street, hoping the fog provided enough cover to hide him. Colin flattened himself against the wall of the hardware store before leaping to the roof with little effort.

A black SUV sped out of the fog, screeching to a stop just a few feet from where Colin had been crouching moments before. Seven agents spilled out, five were wearing tactical clothing and carrying large guns.

If this is the kind of security required for a town-hall meeting, I wonder what's necessary for the monthly sewing club meeting and soup swap?

Keeping the town hall in view, he easily cleared the gap between the hardware store and the bakery. The lingering smell of bread filled his nostrils, and he suddenly craved food. He pushed the feeling aside, much to the disappointment of his stomach, and tried to decide whether he'd really thought this through.

His plan had consisted of getting to the bakery roof and then jumping to one of the town hall second-floor windows. How to get through the window was a small yet essential part of his plan he'd failed to take into consideration. All the windows appeared to be closed, so crashing through them would no doubt raise too much attention. Not to mention, he didn't really know the limitations of his powers. If he ended up with a shard of glass in his head, would it kill him?

Colin started to panic. Maybe he couldn't do this.

Looking closer, he noticed the town hall roof was arched.

Maybe there's a skylight?

Thinking fast, Colin decided he could easily make the jump to the roof and then climb up and over to see if there was a skylight he could either pry open or at least use to take a look inside.

Judging the distance, he took a running jump and landed about half way up the arched roof on black tiles that turned out to be wet and slippery. Unable to get a handhold, he quickly slid straight off the roof, plummeting toward the ground with all the grace of a brick. Colin's heart raced; his skin burned.

I'm falling! Will this kill me? Is this how I die?

A calm realization that he would be fine came over him, like the wolf inside was trying to reassure him. Colin twisted in the air and landed in a squat on the ground. His muscles were tense, but other than that, he seemed okay.

"Hey, you!"

A flashlight shone directly at Colin as a man in a dark suit came around the back corner of the building, probably alerted by the clattering on the roof. This must be the agent at the back door.

Which means there's no one guarding the back door.

As Colin turned and ran, he could hear the agent speaking into his radio.

"It's just a kid. I'm in pursuit."

Colin ducked around the front of the bakery, checked the street to make sure no one was within sight, and then jumped back up to the roof. He peeked back over to see the agent chasing no one through the fog.

Colin ran to the rear of the building, jumped down to the ground, and made for the back door of the town hall. As expected, it was unguarded.

***

Colin quickly found the stairs to the interior balcony. He stopped periodically to listen for the sounds of radio communication, but other than a couple of agents checking in and the general hum of people in the main hall, he didn't hear anything out of the ordinary.

He reached the balcony, which, fortunately, was mostly dark and provided a lot of shadow cover for him to lurk around. Finding a dark corner, Colin crouched low, able to see the main stage and the first couple of rows of the audience but not the entire hall.

But that didn't matter. Colin could hear and smell everything, and that's all he needed.

Colin closed his eyes and let his senses roam free. He found if he concentrated hard enough, he could build a mental picture of the room based on the voices and smells. Some people he recognized easily; others he was less sure about. Principal Hebert was there, standing somewhere in the center of the room, speaking in his low baritone voice with Dr. Flint.

His grandmother shuffled down the middle of the room. Her smell was unmistakable. He recognized other members of the community: the goth twins' mom, Mrs. Cross, seemed to move quickly from one place to another; Mrs. Davenport, the substitute teacher, was there; she smelled nervous; Mr. Byron from the gas station was speaking in a low, hushed tone about the weather and missing the sun. Even Mr. Dugan, Gareth's dad, was present. He had the same garbage smell as his son. Colin could only imagine what their house was like.

Mr. Winter was definitely somewhere in the room, but it was impossible to pinpoint his location; the smell of his aftershave made it seem like he was everywhere at once. Why had the man suddenly taken such a keen interest in drowning himself in aftershave? Colin could only assume he was trying to get a date. Or maybe some woman had lost her grip on reason and logic and had already agreed to date him. It seemed unlikely.

Mr. Emerson stepped onto the stage, and Colin snapped his eyes open to watch him.

Mr. Emerson walked over to the podium and tapped the microphone to make sure it was on. A woman Colin didn't recognize, dressed in a dark suit, sat at a nearby table with a laptop and seemed to be transcribing the meeting.

"Your attention, everyone," said Mr. Emerson, "We had a small incident outside with an unidentified teenager, but he appears to have vacated the area. Other than that, the downtown area is now secure, and I'd like to get the meeting started if you can please take your seats."

The gentle hum of talking dissipated, replaced with the creaking of chairs as people sat down.

What surprised Colin most were the people who took the seats on stage.

Principal Hebert took the second chair, presumably leaving the first for Mr. Emerson, which wasn't entirely out to left field as Hebert was a prominent member of the community. The second was more of a surprise as Colin's grandmother shuffled onto the stage and took the seat next to the hulking principal. Next to him, the tiny woman looked like something Principal Hebert could eat and still leave room for a main course, dessert, and coffee.

Why is she on stage?

The thought was fleeting as the last person hopped up on the stage and sat down next to Colin's grandmother.

Becca?

She looked beautiful, as usual, dressed in dark clothing with her fiery red hair tied back. What was she doing here? Didn't she tell him she was turning in early?

It wasn't like Colin was exactly telling the whole truth either. But why was she on stage?

"I'd like to call to order the meeting of the township of

Elkwood," said Mr. Emerson into the microphone. "Please let the record state that a security sweep has been made, our cover is intact, and we're ready to proceed. I'd like to welcome Captain Hebert, Beatrice Strauss, and Rebecca to the stage to assist with the meeting this evening."

Captain Hebert?

"As you're all aware," continued Mr. Emerson, "the last meeting was cut short after a new predatory creature was detected in the area. We believe this same creature is responsible for the death of one of our local teenagers, Sam Bale. Sam was a normal member of our community, and I know you're all anxious to know the details of the events and how the hunt is proceeding."

So there it was. Silas was the reason the last town meeting ended early, and they blame him for Sam's death. But it wasn't him!

Mr. Emerson continued. "First we need to take care of the usual business. Mrs. Strauss, if you'll please give us an update."

Mr. Emerson bent the microphone down to reach Colin's grandmother as she shuffled her way forward. The woman could barely see over the podium.

"The weather spells remain intact, and the coverage protecting Elkwood remains at full strength," reported Colin's grandmother. "I've been keeping an eye on the town but haven't been able to locate the creature that Commander Emerson will be speaking about. As some of the more educated among you know, in order to maintain full protection and invisibility, I can only see one small section of the town at a time, making searching slow and difficult."

Colin was officially freaking out. Commander Emerson? Weather spells? His grandmother searching the town?

His grandmother shuffled back to her seat and sat down.

"Thank you, Mrs. Strauss," said Mr. Emerson. "We were originally scheduled to discuss Mrs. Strauss mentoring one of our younger community members to begin sharing her responsibility and eventually take over. Due to recent events, that item will be moved to next month's meeting."

Mr. Emerson shuffled some papers in front of him. "Now let's get to the subject at hand so we can dispense with the rumors. We have a werewolf in Elkwood."

Murmurs arose from the crowd. Some people were scared, others smelled of concern, and somewhere in the room, Colin noted, there were a few faint whiffs of excitement.

"Our last meeting ended when I received a call that a werewolf had been detected within the town limits. We tracked it but couldn't contain it. We believe it was hit by a car on the old logging road, but it survived and the car was destroyed. We've been unable to locate the driver. As some of the older among us are aware, werewolves are rare, even to a town such as ours. We know relatively little about them, as there have been few recorded interactions. Werewolves are strong, almost unkillable as they can heal quickly, and they're fast. Faster than most things we've cataloged."

"What are your plans for capturing and killing the creature?" asked Mrs. Cross. Colin had never heard her speak before, but she had a very thick European accent.

"Please hold your questions to the end," said Mr. Emerson. "We know these creatures can multiply by spreading the werewolf virus through a bite. We fear this may have already happened in Elkwood."

More murmuring.

"We can only detect the creatures when they're in their true form and even then the results aren't always accurate. Currently, we have at least two werewolves in Elkwood. They could be anywhere. Today we detected the possibility of a third which leads us to believe they're multiplying."

"And what about the boy? What about Sam Bale?" interrupted Mrs. Cross again.

"Mrs. Cross," admonished Mr. Emerson, anger creeping into his voice. "I understand the threat that a werewolf poses to your kind."

Her kind?

"But I ask that you hold your questions to the end! The death of Sam Bale was regrettable, but I assure you we've been doing everything we can to capture the creatures."

"Not doing a great job, are you?" grumbled Mr. Dugan.

"They can transform from human form to werewolf at will. There could be one in this very room, and there's absolutely no way for us to know. We had a team stakeout the crime scene in the hope it would return to the area like predators sometimes do in order to catch it. Unfortunately the scene was contaminated."

Colin noticed that Becca looked uncomfortable.

Understandable since she was one of the people doing the contaminating.

"That's right," broke in Mr. Dugan, "and one of your trigger-happy soldiers shot my son!"

"Gareth Dugan was found at the crime scene and tried to attack one of our containment crew. He was believed to be a potential hostile and was shot as per our mandate, of which you're all aware." Mr. Emerson gestured toward Becca. "Rebecca healed Gareth's wound. It won't even scar. We consulted with other departments around the world this afternoon to gather as much intel on werewolves as possible. Despite their ability to turn other humans into werewolves, their population is quite low. It seems they regulate themselves though we're not sure how."

"They killed my boy!"

Colin hadn't noticed Sam Bale's father in the hall. He was somewhere in the back.

"You told the town he was attacked and killed by a wild animal. He wasn't just attacked. He was eaten! We didn't even have anything left to bury! And what have you done about it?" demanded Mr. Bale. "We were told Elkwood would be a safe place. That's why we moved here. A safe haven where we can all forget our differences, live together, and be protected from the outside world. My people encountered a werewolf back in the late 1800s. They're vicious murderers, and they need to be killed."

"I agree!" said Mrs. Cross.

Others in the audience chimed in their agreement.

"Come to order!" called Mr. Emerson. "Vampires,

sirens, witches, sorcerers, demons, trolls, ogres, fairies, the undead, ghosts, telepaths, shape shifters."

The crowd quieted down.

"Everyone here lives together in harmony alongside our human residents which adds to our safety and cover. We've taken every possible measure to make this a safe place to raise your families despite our differences."

Colin's heart was racing. So this was it. The big secret. Elkwood was some sort of sanctuary for unearthly creatures?

Over the phone, Mr. Emerson had referred to him as normal. Becca had indicated the same thing before he was bitten. This whole time Colin had been living in a town of freaks.

At least I fit in now.

One moment, Mr. Emerson was standing alone at the podium; in the next, Mrs. Cross was suddenly standing on the stage next to Mr. Emerson. She was quite a striking woman with long blond hair, and a muscular figure that was perfectly proportioned. Colin had never really seen her before as she always stayed in the car picking up the twins.

Mrs. Cross pushed Mr. Emerson out of the way, taking control of the microphone. "We deserve justice! In ancient times, werewolves used to hunt vampire-kind for sport. A blood feud existed between our races for years to the point where the mere smell of a werewolf would make us bodily sick. My twin boys were sick at school the other day, unable to explain why. This creature was somewhere in the school! My family demands the right to break the *no kill* law and hunt these creatures ourselves."

The town hall erupted. While some agreed with this course of action, others vocally disagreed, and a few even accused Mrs. Cross of wanting to break the law so she and her kind could feed on humans again. Mr. Emerson shouted for order but was lost in the din.

The mixture of sound began to hurt Colin's head. Becca looked worried, even scared. Colin began to panic.

These people want to kill me!

He reached out with his mind, searching for Silas.

Silas! Silas! Are you there?

Colin? What's the matter?

Where are you?

I'm on the edge of downtown. There are patrols sweeping the streets, so I'm keeping my distance. What did you find out?

What didn't I find out is more like it! There are vampires here! And demons, and telepaths, and witches. I think my grandmother is a witch. I don't know what Becca is, but she's something too. The vampires are asking for permission to hunt and kill you! To kill me!

Did you say telepaths?

Yeah, why?

A singular voice broke through the din of the hall. It was the voice of Mrs. Davenport the substitute teacher.

Sweet, kind, Mrs. Davenport.

"Wait! Stop! All of you! I can hear him. I can hear him! There's one here, in the hall!" she shrieked.

Mr. Emerson shoved Mrs. Cross away from the podium. "Quiet down! Patricia Davenport. Who? Who is here?"

The hall quieted.

Colin, you have to get out of there. If they have a telepath, she'll be able to hear you talking to me.

But it was too late. Colin was frozen. He didn't know what to do.

I ...

Colin! Get out! Get out now!

"He's somewhere in the hall," said Mrs. Davenport. "I can hear his thoughts. He's communicating to another werewolf."

"Where is he? Where!"

"He's ... he's ... "

Mr. Emerson's in-ear radio crackled to life. The sound was tinny, but Colin could make it out.

"Sir, this is Barrows. He's here. He's moving fast. We ... he's at the town hall door."

Colin heard growling and snarling. He ran to the side of the upstairs balcony just in time to see the town hall doors explode off their hinges and splinter inward. People screamed and ran for cover while Mrs. Cross hissed like an angry cat.

Breathing heavily, Silas stood in the doorway in all his full wolf-like glory. Colin looked on in horror.

Silas, get out of here. They'll kill you!

Colin looked around the hall. Most people were trying to get away from the creature at the door. He looked to the stage, noting that Becca had disappeared. His grandmother still sat in her seat looking as calm and unflappable as ever.

Mr. Emerson screamed into the radio microphone on his sleeve. "All operatives, take him down, non-lethal only. Tranquilize the hell out of him!"

Mrs. Cross leaped from the stage and landed in the middle of the hall. She moved with amazing speed, weaving through the scattered chairs, and dived at Silas who jumped out of the way, landing on all fours. He turned to growl at the blond vampire who hissed back.

Operatives spilled through the doorway, guns drawn, before firing all at once. Silas dived out of the way, and tranquilizer darts thudded harmlessly into the wall. Mrs. Cross lunged again at Silas, but instead of moving, the giant wolf creature grabbed her by the hair, swung her around his head once, and threw her back at the operatives who dived out of the way.

Mr. Emerson opened fire, shooting several darts into Silas's back.

Colin's skin began to crawl, and he could feel his own creature fighting to get out. He tried to stay calm, but his heart rate was through the roof and his senses were exploding.

Silas staggered and fell forward as more agents approached and unloaded more tranquilizer darts into his prone body.

"No!" shouted Colin.

I'll tear them apart!

A surge of anger as if a family member had been attacked.

Someone grabbed his arm.

Colin spun around, breathing heavily, and came face to face with Becca.

"Colin, your eyes, your teeth!"

Colin ran his tongue around the inside of his mouth. His teeth had grown. He expected his eyes were shining that golden amber color again.

C-Colin. G ... get out. N-now.

"I know where they're taking him." said Becca. "You can't help him now, but I know where he'll be."

Was Becca trying to help? Or was it a trick?

Colin looked back to the hall. Silas was no longer moving. Agents had begun securing him with netting. Colin looked to the stage to see his grandmother staring in his direction. She nodded her head to the side.

Is she telling me to leave?

Colin allowed Becca to lead him from the balcony, down the staircase, through the kitchen, out the back door, and into the night.

Chapter Fifteen

Granny Storm

Colin ran after Becca at what felt like a snail's pace; the night was exploding in chaos behind them. Colin could hear the townsfolk as they fled the downtown area. More operatives were converging on the town hall, probably as a precaution, in case Silas woke up and started eating people.

Colin's mind was spinning with all the new information he'd learned in such a short space of time. "Becca, where are we going?"

Becca didn't answer or stop. They reached the school, and Colin followed her around the back of the building to the football field. Arriving at the bleachers, Becca finally stopped and sat down heavily, out of breath. Colin hadn't broken a sweat.

"Can you please stop pacing?" said Becca. "You're making me nervous."

Colin hadn't realized he had been stalking back and forth in front of Becca. He was anxiously fighting an overwhelming urge to rip off his clothes, change, and go back to the town hall. He stopped pacing.

"What were you doing at the town hall, Colin? You're the other werewolf, aren't you? And he's the one that bit you? That's why you've been weird all week. You've been changing! That's why you feel different to me, isn't it? Are you going to answer me?"

Colin couldn't decide whether she was sad or angry or a dynamic mixture of the two.

"Answer me!" demanded Becca.

I'm going to call that angry.

"If I could get a word in edgewise, I'd be happy to start answering your questions," said Colin, smiling. Becca offered a reluctant smile in return.

"Colin, you're a werewolf."

"Yes."

"Did you … did you kill Sam Bale?"

Now it was Colin's turn to be angry. Bad enough wondering if he was a killer without the girl he liked thinking it too. "Oh, come on, Becca! Do you really th—"

"It's a legitimate question. I just found out the guy I've been crushing on is a werewolf!"

"I just found out that the girl I've been crushing on is a … what are you anyway?"

He could feel and smell the anger return.

"I'm a necromancer!"

"You fall asleep a lot?"

Her anger subsided a little.

"That's narcolepsy."

"So you … ?"

"I bring people back from the dead. And I can heal almost any sort of injury."

"Creepy."

"Says the dog boy?"

Ha! Good one.

"Zombie queen!"

"Go find a ball. We can play fetch."

"So do you and Satan hang out?"

"Now I know why you always smell like wet dog."

Colin couldn't think of a good comeback. So he chose the obvious thing to do in such an awkward situation with the girl of your dreams.

Colin kissed her.

It was a passionate first-time kiss with a limited amount of drool. Colin rated it a ten, but he really didn't have anything else to compare it to.

Becca looked a little confused. Or was she happy?

"What? Did I do it wrong? Was it the wrong time? I thought we had a bit of a thing going there and I saw an opportunity and I may have been panicking a little. To be honest, I'm panicking again now and—"

Becca kissed Colin.

It was better this time, less drool.

"Wow," said Colin.

His skin was tingling again, but he felt in control. For the moment, at least. "Did you say you've been crushing on me?" Colin suddenly remembered. "Since when?"

Becca shrugged. "Since a while. I don't break into everyone's house in the middle of the night, ya know?"

"Wow," repeated Colin.

"What?"

"Well, it's just a funny thought. I mean, getting bit by a werewolf and worrying that I may have eaten a classmate while being hunted by your father, well, it may have been the best thing that ever happened to me."

Becca smiled, the rest of her anger subsiding. "So you didn't kill Sam Bale?"

"I'm almost 95% sure that I didn't. Everything was a bit of a blur the night I was bitten. Silas didn't kill him either. He came here to hunt the other werewolf in town."

"And who is the other werewolf?"

"We haven't figured it out yet. Although, all this time you've known about all of this. Elkwood, the wolf attack. Everything! You knew there was a werewolf in town, and you still took us out to that crime scene. Do you have a death wish?"

"My powers emerged at a young age; I guess death doesn't scare me like it does other people. I've literally seen the other side."

"What's it like?"

"It's all rainbow-colored and smells like freshly baked cookies."

"Seriously?"

"No, not even close."

They both laughed.

"Becca, where are they taking Silas?"

"They'll take him to the compound. It's the old army base beyond the forest. They hold the more volatile subjects up there while they study their behavior."

"We have to go get him. He's not a bad werewolf. He's

the balance! He's the one who keeps the bad werewolves at bay. It's some sort of life mission of his."

"Colin, I'm all for breaking your werewolf daddy out of the top-secret government base guarded by trained soldiers who carry very high-powered weaponry and are reinforced with magic."

"But?"

"No but." Becca smiled that smile that Colin loved.

"How do we get there?"

"I could ride you?" suggested Becca, her face flushing. "Would that be weird? Honestly, that just slipped out. I mean, you could change and then I could … just kill me now. Bite my head off or something."

Colin laughed. "I don't know where I'm going. You'll need to direct me."

"I can do that."

There was an element of risk. Silas had said they could track werewolves in their wolf form but then, there was no other fast way to the base. Colin hoped they were too preoccupied with Silas to worry about him. He kicked off his shoes, and stripped down to his underwear.

"Would you, uh, would you mind turning around?" said Colin.

Becca snapped around quickly. "Sorry!"

"It's just that this is only the second time I've changed, and I really don't think it's something you'll want to see. There's a lot of stretching and bones clicking. It's actually kinda gross. Oh, and can you bring my clothes? I'll need something to wear once we're up there."

Becca nodded.

"Okay. Here we go."

Colin wasn't sure where to start. He had voluntarily brought on a change from werewolf to human, but he'd only done it the other way once and it wasn't by choice. Reaching out with his mind, he searched for Silas but couldn't find him anywhere.

Silas, are you out there?

Nothing.

C'mon, Colin. Think wolfy thoughts!

It didn't work.

Becca had collected all his clothes and folded them neatly into a bundle. "How's it going over there?" said Becca.

"It's not. I don't know how to do this. I must be the worst werewolf in history."

"How did you change the first time?"

"I was overcome with a strong emotion."

"What emotion?"

Crap.

"It's hard to explain."

"What's hard to explain?"

"Shh," said Colin.

Something was moving in front of the school. Colin could hear light footsteps. Then the faint crackle of a radio.

"Oh no."

"What?"

"Good evening, Mr. Strauss," said the booming voice of Principal Hebert.

Lights flicked on from several different directions. Focused on his change, Colin hadn't heard the team of agents or guards or whatever they were until it was too late. He was also suddenly very aware that he was only wearing his underwear.

Colin quickly counted ten different lights, each one mounted to a rifle and trained on Colin. He could hear Becca's heart begin to race. Fortunately, he could hear everyone else's heartbeats, and they were fast. These men were nervous. Colin tried to not take too much joy in the potentially dangerous situation, but it made him feel kind of good. These people were afraid of him.

"Mr. Strauss," said Principal Hebert, who was also carrying a rifle, "you were sighted at the town hall meeting this evening. And now here you are, practically naked behind the school with Ms. Emerson. Quite unexpected."

"We're … we're dating," tried Colin lamely.

"Mr. Strauss, would you mind explaining why you were at the town hall tonight, why you suddenly have muscles, and why you …never mind. Let's just get to the point. Are you, Colin Strauss, a werewolf?"

Colin laughed uncomfortably. "Me? A werewolf?"

Say no, say no, say no, say no.

"Yes," said Colin, "yes, I am."

It wasn't some macho move to suddenly admit to what he was, it was actually nothing like that. Colin simply didn't feel ashamed. Being a werewolf gave him a certain amount of power, and frankly, he loved it. An even bigger thrill ran through him when several of the men with guns took a short step backward at his declaration.

"I really thought you were joking when you told me you were late because you had stolen a car and seen a giant wolf creature in your shower. It never occurred to me that plain old Colin Strauss was a killer."

"Woah, now wait a moment, Mr. Hebert," said Colin. "I didn't kill Sam Bale."

"That remains to be seen."

"I'll take it from here, Hebert, you great buffoon," said the tiny figure of Colin's grandmother as she pushed her way past two agents with guns and walked straight past Principal Hebert.

"Grandmother," said Colin.

The blind woman stopped a few feet in front of Colin.

"Mrs. Strauss—" tried Principal Hebert.

"Oh, shut your trap and let me do my job! Now listen here, boy. I'm going to read your mind. And we'll see exactly what's going on up there in that sad excuse you call a brain."

So this was how they had found Colin, his grandmother had tipped them off. He had never despised the woman more than he did at that very moment.

Oh, calm your feisty little mind down!

It was his grandmother's voice, in his head.

Can you hear me?

Yes, and you can hear me. Now listen carefully to me, my boy. I know moving here hasn't been easy for you. Now that you can see Elkwood for what it is, I expect you can understand why I wasn't thrilled when your parents decided to send you here. It's a dangerous place, and these idiots with the guns don't know any better. They're fumbling around catching creatures and monsters and all sorts of other things they don't understand.

Grandmother, I didn't kill Sam Bale.

I know that, you great fool. I'm in your mind, and I see everything. Now, one day you and I will have a long talk about stealing cars and sneaking out at night, but today is not that day. Tell me, do you know who killed the Bale boy?

No. Silas and I have been trying to figure it out. All we know is that it wasn't either of us.

And this Silas, he's a good werewolf. I can see it in your mind. You and the Emerson girl were going to go after him?

He's innocent. He's the one that came here to catch the werewolf that killed Sam Bale. Whatever they're going to do with him up at that base, he doesn't deserve it.

I'm going to buy you some time. You need to turn yourself into that thing, and you and the girl go and free that man. I may work for these idiots, but I don't approve of their methods, nor do I like people pointing guns at my grandson. Even if he is rude. Interesting. But rude.

Colin couldn't help himself; he was smiling inside. He glanced back to see Becca slowly backing a few feet away.

I tried to change. I couldn't do it.

Try harder.

That's it? That's your advice? Aren't you a witch or something? I would have thought you being a witch would give you, I don't know, some sort of ancient wisdom?

Oh, I'm not just a witch …

Colin's grandmother smiled. It was a ghastly picture to behold. Colin had never seen it happen. The creases in her face must have felt terribly unnatural to bend into such a position.

... I'm a very powerful witch.

Lightning tore across the night sky. The ground began to shake and thunder boomed from the heavens.

"What are you doing?" said Principal Hebert. "Keep your weapons on the boy."

A few of the men lost their footing as the earth moved beneath them, lightning striking in rapid succession around the school. Several others dropped their guns and headed for cover.

"Stop this right now!" demanded Principal Hebert. But it was clear that Colin's grandmother had no intention of stopping.

A wind began to roar around the school, and Colin dropped to the ground to keep from being knocked off his feet.

"I said stop this right now, Beatrice!" Principal Hebert's voice was lost to the wind. A tornado erupted where he stood and threw him across the ground. He regained his footing and screamed into his radio mic. "Take the boy down. Take him now!"

Even though most of the men had fled, Colin clearly heard several weapons being loaded through the chaotic storm.

Now, Colin. Do it now!

Colin took the fear of being shot, the fear of the storm raging around him, and the fear he'd always felt for his grandmother and pushed them together inside him. The creature within began to wake, but it wasn't happening fast enough!

A gun fired, the *zing* of a tranquilizer dart whizzing past his ear, and that was the final much-needed push.

The wolf inside him sensed the danger and erupted like a string of explosions. Instead of his skin tingling, Colin experienced a brief, sharp pain, bones quickly snapping into place and muscles expanding as claws flicked out of his fingers and toes. Hair exploded from his body while his mouth extended into a snout and his teeth grew. In a split second, he was a werewolf again, and he felt the power surge through him. It felt amazing. He growled loudly.

Colin paused a brief moment to truly look at his grandmother. This not so frail lady was the guardian of the entire town. She kept it all a secret by never allowing the sun to shine in Elkwood. She was hiding the town from the rest of the world.

Gran, what about you?

Don't be a baby. I can take care of myself.

Another shot fired and Colin quickly ducked and growled. He turned, grabbed Becca who had been holding onto one of the school picnic tables to keep from being blown over, and threw her onto his back as he dropped onto all fours. "Hold on," Colin tried to say, but it came out as more of a growl.

Hold on, he thought instead. Becca gripped two handfuls of the thick hair on Colin's back as he accelerated into the night. The ground flew beneath him as he cleared the football field in seconds, leaving the school, the men who were shooting at him, and his all-powerful witch of a grandmother behind.

Chapter Sixteen

Attempted Rescue

Colin kept a steady pace with Becca giving him the occasional direction. At one point Colin caught himself with his tongue hanging out the side of his mouth. He couldn't help it. The running, the wind rippling through his hair, a beautiful girl on his back—it was a dream come true.

A strange dream, but still a dream.

"What did you say?" said Becca.

Colin found that it was easy to project into Becca's mind. She seemed to hear his thoughts loud and clear though he had trouble turning it off. He assumed it was something that took practice.

So much made sense now. The weird tingly feeling when Becca had touched him was her poking around in his body. His grandmother was a powerful witch who could control the weather. Figuring he had a captive audience, Colin asked Becca question after question as they made their way through the forest.

How are you involved, and why were you on stage at the meeting?

"I'm the resident healer," said Becca. "After we stumbled upon Gareth at the crime scene the other night, he was shot by one of my dad's men when he tried to escape. I healed him."

That's why he hugged you at school?

"Well, I did pull a bullet out of him."

Have you ever brought anyone back from the dead?

"I'm still young in my powers. I've only done small things. Just healing Gareth put me out of commission for two days. I can't imagine what it'd take from me bringing someone back from the dead."

What about the other kids in our school? Are they all witches and monsters?

"Some of them are normal, like you. Or like you were before you went and got all hairy. When the government set up shop in Elkwood, they put certain enchantments in place to hide the unusual traits of people in town. Only the monsters and freaks like you and I can see everyone for what they truly are.

Why Elkwood? Why not set up elsewhere? Where no normal people are even around.

"It's all part of the cover. Your grandmother is the first line of defense. If anyone ever accidentally wandered into town, they wouldn't see anything out of the ordinary. Some of the humans here are also here for a reason. Mr. Winter is a biological consultant for my father for example. Other than that, there's nothing special about him. The same with Principal Hebert. He's an ex-marine and the caretaker of the—"

Colin swerved to avoid a low branch and Becca almost lost her balance.

Sorry. Okay, so dish the goods. Who's what?

This question had been bugging him since the town hall. Now that Colin was a creature himself, he wanted to know what everyone else was.

Thunder rumbled somewhere behind them.

"Well the twins—"

Obviously vampires. I saw their mother at the town hall. She's a real piece of work.

"You're going to want to watch her. Vampires have some sort of ancient feud with werewolves. Mrs. Cross is over thirteen hundred years old."

She looks good for her age.

"Apparently your smell makes them physically ill. I don't know how you're ever going to be around the goth twins again unless you can cover your scent somehow."

A stray thought wandered through Colin's mind looking for a connection.

Scent ...

"What was that?"

Nothing, just something you said. So what about Tori?

"Oh sure, ask about the smoking hot girl."

Just curious. Just idle curiosity, nothing else.

"Well, she's not that hot. She's a siren. An ancient race that lures men to their deaths and then eats them."

That does make her less appealing but also explains a lot.

"Gareth Dugan is part ogre. Jillian Saunders in our geography class is a full-blown demon. Kevin Hadfield is a swamp creature. Matthew Price is part dragon."

Matthew Price? Tiny, asthmatic Matthew Price?

"The one and same."

And Jeremy? What's he?

"I have no idea. He's classified."

Classified? What's that mean?

"It means he's dangerous and has been magicked into not knowing what he is for the safety of others."

Does that happen a lot?

"The government prefers integration over imprisonment, so yes. Sometimes it doesn't work though. They're still learning as they go. Dad took his position here after I was discovered to have powers."

"And he runs the whole place?"

"He tries."

Colin skidded to a stop, and Becca slid from his back. They were standing below a vertical rock face that ran straight up for around fifty feet. At the top was a wire fence with barbed wire on top.

So how do we get in?

"I've only been here twice, and both times I used the front door, but I don't think that's an option for us. Can you climb this wall?"

Can a duck poop in the woods? Wait, that's not right. Isn't it a bear or a tree? The short answer is yes.

"Can you carry me and climb?"

Sure.

Colin easily picked Becca up with two hairy, clawed hands and placed her on his back.

Hold on tight.

Becca held fast to his neck as Colin stood up on

two legs. Studying the wall, he carefully crouched, then launched himself into the air. He easily reached the halfway point and dug his powerful claws into the rock face. Finding some footing on a ledge, Colin balanced and threw himself upward again, this time clearing the top ledge. He jumped over the fence, easily clearing the barbed wire, and landed lightly on the other side. Becca let out a low squeal that could have been fear, excitement, or both and slid from his back.

They were in a large yard stacked with canisters and crates that looked like it was used for storage. Colin couldn't hear or smell anyone else. To the right there was a long low building and to the left an aircraft hangar. A road at the opposite end of the yard spiralled down and away from the buildings; Colin assumed it led to the front gate.

"You should change. They have a group of psychics working for them that can sense your kind in wolf form."

Colin quickly pictured himself as a human. Again, it almost bordered on painful to let go of the power. To make it worse, he could feel the wolf inside him fighting against the change. There was danger here, and the wolf could sense it. Reluctantly, it finally gave up, and Colin was human again, resting on all fours, watching as the hair around him disintegrated into nothing.

Becca threw his clothes down and turned her back while Colin dressed.

"So, what now?" said Colin.

"We need to get down to the cell blocks. That hangar has an elevator that will take us there, but I don't have a key card."

"Where is everyone?"

"Probably observing your friend. It's the first werewolf they've ever seen. The prison section is deep in the mountain. This section of the base doesn't take much protecting, so there are never many people around."

"Wait, I hear someone."

Becca and Colin ducked down as a small door inset to the large hangar door swung open and an armed guard stepped out.

"What's he doing?" whispered Becca.

Colin listened carefully, took in a deep breath, allowing his mind to illuminate the base in a wash of color. He heard the flick of a lighter and then a deep intake of breath followed by a satisfied sigh. "He's smoking."

"Is he alone?"

"I don't hear anyone else. Will he have a key card?"

"Yes. Can you take him?"

Colin hadn't really thought about it. It's not like he'd been in a fight since he acquired these new powers, but he felt like he could easily rip someone in half. "I think so?"

Becca tilted her head. "You don't sound that confident."

"I'm still new at all this. I don't know what I can and can't do at this point."

Becca let out an exasperated sigh. "I'll take care of him."

"Wait … what?" Before Colin could finish Becca had already slipped around the cargo container and was casually walking across the yard toward the guard.

Colin panicked. He moved fast, diving quickly from one container to another, getting closer to the guard.

He paused and looked over at Becca, who had reached the thirty-something man. Colin could easily hear their conversation.

"Hi," said Becca. "It's uh, James, right?"

"David," said the guard.

"Right. David. You know who—"

"What are you doing here, Ms. Emerson?" interrupted David.

"My dad didn't call ahead? He's getting so forgetful since he turned forty-five."

"I'm going to need to call this in. You're not supposed—"

Becca reached out and touched the guard's face.

"… to be, ugh, ehh, ahh."

Colin felt a stab of jealousy and moved without thinking. He ran toward the guard and tackled him into the hangar door, denting it.

"Colin, what is wrong with you?" said Becca.

"No need to thank me."

"Thank you? I had it under control. He was unconscious already. I can do that!"

"You can make people unconscious? How?"

Becca waved her hands in the air. "I'm a witch, dummy. Remember?"

"So I just tackled an unconscious man?"

"Yeah, you tackled him hard."

"I think I broke some of his ribs."

"Bad dog."

"Funny."

Becca knelt by the guard, unhooking a plain white card from his belt. "Let's go."

***

Colin decided that this must be the most unguarded army base in all of the US. He and Becca made it into the hangar, through two sets of security doors, and the elevator with no problems whatsoever. It was like a ghost town.

The massive elevator was like nothing Colin had seen before. You could easily fit at least forty werewolves in here and still have room.

Uhmm.

Silas?

Colargh.

Silas, are you okay? I'm coming to get you out.

Baarggh. Idargh.

You're not making any sense. You must still be groggy from the tranquilizers. I'll be there soon.

There was nothing.

Silas?

Total silence.

The elevator shuddered to a stop, the digital readout showing a descent of fifteen floors. The large doors hissed open, and Colin and Becca carefully stepped out into a hallway lined with metal doors. With Becca leading the way, Colin stopped at the first door and peered through a small window set into the door. The room was bathed in red light, and three people sat cross-legged in a circle with black bags over their heads. They were rocking back and forth.

"Yoga?" guessed Colin with a smirk.

"Funny. That's Curly, Larry, and Moe, or the Three Stooges. These are the psychics they've been using to track you and your friend. From what I've heard, they only seem to be able to locate you when you're in your wolf form and even then it doesn't seem to be exact."

They continued down the hallway until Becca stopped at the last door on the right and swiped the key card through a reader. The door clicked open, and they went inside.

It was dark, but Colin could make everything out perfectly. It was a laboratory. A very clean, sterile-smelling laboratory. Becca moved to the wall, clicked a button, and a panel inside the wall flashed to life.

"How'd you do that?"

"They bring me up here every time a solider gets hurt. The base has all sorts of gadgets. Dad doesn't talk about it much, but I've heard some of the guards say that the government didn't spare any expense when they built this place."

"Why keep a town like Elkwood running? Why not just kill all the weird creatures?"

"Because there's power here. What if the world goes to war? What if we're invaded by aliens?"

"It'd help to have a bunch of powerful creatures in your back pocket."

"Exactly. Come look."

Colin approached the window, which overlooked a large warehouse floor. It suddenly became clear where all the guards were.

There were around two hundred men and women on the warehouse floor congregated around the unconscious hulking figure of a werewolf.

"Silas."

Silas' hands and feet were chained to the ground, and Colin could see his chest was rising and falling heavily. Straining the limits of his abilities to hear through the reinforced wall, he managed to pick up the occasional words.

"We got him."

"A real life werewolf."

"—pay for what he did."

"Nothing but a beast."

"What are they doing?" said Colin.

"They're observing. Catching a werewolf is a big thing for these guys. In their minds, they've caught the killer beast."

"But they think he's the killer. He's not. The killer is still out there somewhere."

"Or in here with me?"

Colin didn't answer. It was still a possibility.

"I thought we might be able to figure a way to get him out of there, but now I'm not so sure," said Becca.

"This is ridiculous. Is that everyone? I mean all the guards?"

"Most of them."

"Which means Elkwood is unprotected. The other werewolf could be down there right now, but no one is there because they think they already caught him."

"What are you saying, Colin?"

"We need to tell someone. We have to let someone know that Silas isn't the killer. And that I'm not the killer. That there's a third werewolf in Elkwood."

Becca looked at Colin with ... what?

Admiration? Smells like watermelon.

"I have an idea," said Becca. "I think I know who we can talk to."

Becca took Colin's hand, something he never grew tired of, and led him out of the lab and back to the elevator. The large doors swished open.

The numbers on the elevator control panel went to twenty. Another button beneath the numbered ones was blank. Becca pressed it, and the elevator began to drop. "This will feel a little strange."

The elevator picked up speed.

"What do you mean 'strange'?"

"We're going to visit the soothsayer."

"I don't know what that means."

The elevator was moving faster. Colin felt lighter as the effects of gravity lessened. "Becca," said Colin, "what's happening?"

The elevator glowed brightly as a loud, throbbing noise thrummed painfully through Colin's wolf ears. Becca had to shout to be heard.

"The soothsayer doesn't live on this plane of existence. We have to go to a different reality to see him!"

"What?"

In a flash of blinding light, Colin felt ill as the world folded in on itself. The pressure in his head was unbelievably painful. And it got worse. He was falling. Or sinking. Or flying. He wasn't sure. Vaguely aware of Becca shouting somewhere close by but he couldn't get past the feeling of being shoved through a very thin tube that was in no way made for his size and shape.

Finally it became too much, and Colin passed out.

Chapter Seventeen

The Creepy Floating Dude

Colin woke up to Becca slapping him repeatedly. "I'm awake, I'm awake. You can stop hitting me."

"Sorry about that. The first time you take the elevator to the bottom floor, it messes with your senses a little bit."

Colin blinked a few times and looked around. They were in a large, cave-like stone chamber, candles flickering all around. There was a single stone table in the center, and from what Colin could see, no way in and no way out.

"Becca, where are we?"

Becca pulled Colin to his feet. His stomach felt queasy, and moving around wasn't helping matters.

"It's hard to explain," said Becca. "This is an antechamber between our world and a parallel world that lives beneath ours."

"So, this is hell?"

"I like to think of it as hell's penthouse suite," said a voice vaguely familiar to Colin. Floating a few feet off the ground behind Colin and Becca was the man Colin had seen in the alleyway the night Silas had bit him. The floating man was still wearing the same shabby brown cloak and hood that covered his body from head to toe. "Becca," said Colin, "is that man really floating?"

"I'm a witch, you're a werewolf, we just travelled to a different plane of existence, and you're surprised by the creepy floating dude?"

The man tilted his hooded head to the side. "Creepy? Becca, you've never called me creepy before."

The voice was hollow and cold.

"You live just above Hell and predict the future. And you float. And you're a demon. Creepy doesn't sum all that up, Charles?"

"Charles?" said Colin.

"Sorry," apologized Becca. "Colin, this is Charles. He's the soothsayer. He's a sort of political refugee from Hell. He works for the US government in exchange for living a peaceful life."

"A peaceful life that I'm not allowed to leave," said Charles.

"I've seen you before though, outside," Colin accused. "That night in the alleyway. You told me I had to go or I'd be late."

"And I see from that magnificent beast inside you that you were right on time. You're welcome."

"Thanks, I think. But how did I see you there if you can't leave?"

"I can send an astral projection of myself into Elkwood if there's reason enough. Although Commander Emerson isn't a fan of me doing so."

"Charles," said Becca, "if you knew Colin would be bitten, why didn't you tell my father?"

"If I did that, you both wouldn't be here." Charles floated around the two teenagers and over to the table, then lightly perched on the edge. "My gift is not an exact science. When I look into a person, I can see all the possibilities of every decision clearly laid out before me. Sometimes I can see the future. Other times I can see only the present. That night in the alley, I saw Colin make the decision to leave Elkwood, and I saw the creature that would bring him back."

"Silas isn't the killer they think he is," said Colin.

"I know that. The killer is still in Elkwood. He's planning on killing again in just a few hours. I've seen his victim."

The words settled like ice in Colin's heart but brought a certain amount of relief too.

"I didn't kill Sam Bale."

"No, you didn't. You killed a deer. And then you ate it."

Embarrassed, Colin looked at Becca. "I was hungry."

"Your friend, Silas, will not be able to prevent the murder," said Charles, "but you, Colin, we can expect some great things from you, I think."

Colin turned to Becca. "Does he ever speak normally? Straightforward? To the point?" He walked slowly toward Charles. "I don't know who or what you are. In the last week I've been beaten up, tried to skip town, bitten by a werewolf, turned into a werewolf, which I admit isn't that bad, and discovered that I live in a town full of freaks. I need to know two things: who the killer is, and how do I stop him?"

Charles pulled back the sleeves of his shabby coat to reveal skin burned beyond the help of any antiseptic cream. Hands with long, black nails reached up, pushing back his hood.

Stay calm. It's just a scary-looking demon. A scary, horrific, terrifying, the stuff nightmares are made of demon.

And it was.

Charles's face was burned to the point of having no skin whatsoever. Charred patches of sinew and muscle were all that remained. His teeth were black and pointy. Colin tried his best to look into Charles's eyes, or at least he would have if Charles had any eyes to look into. Dark, empty sockets gaped back at Colin who was fighting the urge to throw up.

"Beautifully hideous, aren't I? This is what a millennium in hell will do for you. As I said, my power is not an exact science. I can only see possible outcomes."

"Then you know who the killer is," said Becca. "You must have seen him."

"Not true, young one. Despite my best efforts, I haven't been able to find the werewolf who killed the young boy and will be killing again very soon unless something is done about it."

"If you haven't seen him, how do you know—?"

"The victim," Colin realized. "You said you've seen the victim?"

"Yes," said the demon matter-of-factly. "Young Ms.

Becca Emerson here is the next victim. She will die tomorrow morning during first period."

The color drained from Becca's face. Colin placed his hands on her shoulders. "You heard the creepy demon. We know now we can stop it from happening. We have to tell your father."

"Sadly that won't work," said Charles. "I've seen the possibilities. I've seen the outcomes. Mr. Emerson will not listen and will not believe either of you. Or me for that matter."

"Why not?" said Colin.

"You'll see in a moment. My best advice is that you figure out who the killer is before it's too late. It's your only chance." Charles smiled a wide smile, parts of his face cracking a little.

"You're enjoying this!" accused Colin.

"Well, I *am* a demon. A nice demon but still a demon."

The area in the cave behind Colin and Becca began to shimmer and stretch as if reality was trying to rip itself open. Then it did. A tear opened, and out stepped a furious-looking Mr. Emerson followed closely by two armed guards. One of them drew a pistol and shot Colin in the leg.

"What the—" was all Colin could manage before everything went hazy. He looked down to see a dart sticking out of his thigh just above the knee. The wolf inside him growled, but the change wouldn't come. The tranquilizer was slowing his heartbeat.

"No!" said Becca to her father. "I'm going to die. The werewolf will kill me. Charles has seen it!"

"Impossible! We've got both werewolves now. Our

psychics no longer believe there's a third. Sgt. Sampson," said Mr. Emerson to the guard on his right, "escort my daughter home and then make sure she gets to school in the morning. Don't let her out of your sight."

"Yes, sir!" said Sgt. Sampson and escorted Becca out through the tear in reality that didn't appear to be going anywhere.

"Wargargalagagaga," mumbled Colin, falling to his knees, as the tranquilizers began to take full effect.

"And you," said Mr. Emerson to Charles. "I'm sick of your false information. First, you can't find the damn werewolf, even when it shows up at the town hall meeting, and then you didn't bother to warn us about old Mrs. Strauss going weather crazy on us. Or that my daughter and her werewolf boyfriend would try sneaking into our secret army base."

"Blarghfreend," said Colin and smiled. At least he thought he smiled. What he was probably doing was drooling.

"At this point," said Charles, "I'm inclined to tell you that you're making a terrible mistake and that your daughter is in terrible danger, but you won't believe me and will simply tell me to shut up and give me a stern warning."

"Shut up. Any more screw-ups like this, and we'll be looking at revoking your sanctuary. Clear?"

"Crystal," said Charles and pulled his hood over his head.

Mr. Emerson pulled a syringe from his pocket and crouched down next to Colin. Colin could now see three Mr. Emersons, and they all looked equally angry.

"That's right. We reviewed the camera footage from outside the base. We know you're a werewolf too. What's your plan? Take over Elkwood? Turn us all into your kind maybe?"

"Balsharts," said Colin, trying hard to fight unconsciousness.

"We'll find out once you wake up. You're probably wondering what's in this." Mr. Emerson held up the syringe filled with a yellowish liquid. "This is an inhibitor. We use it in Elkwood to keep the vampire's bloodlust at a minimum. One of our scientists thought it might have the same effect on werewolves, so we tested it on your friend upstairs, and what do you know? It works. Apparently, this little cocktail will keep you from changing. Maybe it'll cure you altogether. We don't really know. But at the very least, it'll stop you from turning into that creature."

"Splurg," objected Colin. It didn't work.

Colin felt warmth trickle through him as Mr. Emerson jabbed the needle into his neck. The wolf that had been clawing to get out retreated into the shadows of Colin's mind until he couldn't feel its presence anymore.

Someone was dragging him toward the dark tear in reality. Charles the demon was still perched on the stone table.

"Remember my words, Colin Strauss. You know the creature inside you. You're a werewolf in Elkwood. You don't want to get caught. What would you do?"

As darkness edged in around him, Colin thought about the demon's words.

I'd hide.

"Eigh heed," said Colin.

Chapter Eighteen

In the Doghouse

C olin stood in a forest clearing on a bright summer's day, rays of sunlight breaking through the canopy of trees. But he wasn't alone. A massive wolf creature stalked out from behind a nearby bush, coming closer and closer. The sky turned overcast, and the creature circled him.

Colin wasn't afraid, he knew this wolf, it was his friend. He reached out to touch the creature, but no matter how hard he tried, he couldn't. Every time he reached for it, the wolf would be just a little too far away. The wolf creature looked sad that Colin couldn't reach him, and it howled a mournful howl.

***

Colin's eyes snapped open. He was lying on the floor of a prison cell. It was a nice cell, not the kind you see on late-night TV shows.

The back wall was solid metal while the front and sides were made up of thick, shiny metal bars. The cell to his left was empty. Silas lay snoring on the floor in the cell to his right.

Colin stood and walked to the front of the cell. There was no door, so he suspected that the bars must retract or move to let people in or out. The hallway outside was wide, and additional cells lined either side of it. In the middle of the room was a bank of monitors and a single guard gazing casually at them. There were around twelve cells total, and most of them were occupied. Many of the prisoners looked human, though Colin suspected they were anything but.

However, there were a couple that stood out. Across the hall, almost directly across from Colin's cell, was what looked like a small purple dragon. It was the size of a large dog, and it was staring intently at the guard. In the cell next to the dragon was a huge, hulking creature. It looked like a human but at least ten times the size of a normal person. Massive hands gripped the bars, and every so often the creature would bang its head against them.

"Knock it off," called the guard to the massive creature. "And you," he said pointing at the dragon, "stop staring at me, you're freaking me out."

Colin walked over to the bars separating him from Silas. "Silas!" said Colin.

Silas didn't move.

"Silas, come on. It's me, Colin. Please wake up."

Nothing.

"Silas!"

Nope.

"Silas, wake up!"

"Won't do you any good," said the guard from his desk. "We doped him up with so many tranquilizers he'll sleep for a week. Maybe longer."

Silas!

Silas groaned and rolled onto his back. Then he started to drool.

Colin returned to the front of the cell. "Hey, you!" said Colin to the guard. "You have to let me out of here."

The guard laughed a little too enthusiastically. "And why would I do such a thing?"

"Because there's still a werewolf out there and I need to stop it."

"Ha! The Three Stooges already confirmed their earlier predictions of a third werewolf were false and that you two are the only ones of your kind in Elkwood. Which means one of you killed that boy. I don't want to speculate, but I'm thinking you're not going to be seeing the outside world for a long time so you should just make yourself comfortable."

"You can't just lock me up here!"

"Let me ask you something."

"What?"

"Are you in a cell right now?"

"Yes."

"Then I'm pretty sure you're wrong about that not locking up thing." Laughing, the guard turned back to the monitors.

"What time is it?" asked Colin, despair in his voice.

The guard sighed. "It's 7:00 a.m. Now quiet down. I'm reading my horoscope."

Seven a.m.! School starts in less than two hours.

Colin felt helpless. How was he going to find the other werewolf and save Becca? The thought made him angry, and he felt the familiar increase in his heart rate. Skin tingling, the creature inside him began to stir ... then stopped. Colin could still feel the wolf inside. He still felt strong. He could smell the sarcastic guard and the dragon and hear sounds from all over the complex, but he couldn't turn into the wolf creature. Whatever Mr. Emerson injected him with, it was working.

Who could the other werewolf be?

Elkwood wasn't a big town; Colin knew almost everyone. He tried to remember what Charles the demon had said. *What would I do if I was the other werewolf? I'd hide. But how would I hide?*

Colin began to pace back and forth. Silas had come to town looking for the other werewolf. He said he'd tracked it here from California, and that it had already killed.

Colin punched one of the cell bars in frustration, which rang in protest.

"Hey!" said the guard. "Cool it, puppy dog, or we'll have to put you back to sleep. Those bars are pure titanium. You won't be breaking through them anytime soon."

Colin sat down on the cell floor. Ever since he'd started changing, he'd been able to think with such perfect clarity. He could process information quicker, easily filling notebooks full of details about his change into a werewolf. Now it felt like he was trying to think through a fog. Whether it was the effects of the tranquilizer or the injection to suppress his change, it was messing with his mind.

Colin closed his eyes and concentrated, letting his senses spread out through the complex. The cellblock exploded into brilliant colors. He could pick out the guard's heartbeat along with everyone else's. Silas was snoring. Snippets of guard's conversations outside the cellblock filtered in. There was a lot of chatter about the capture of the two werewolves.

"The older guy killed that Bale kid and turned the Strauss kid," said a guard somewhere on the floor above.

"I hear the research department can't wait to get their hands on the werewolves," said another.

A radio communication caught Colin's ear. "They're bringing in the old Strauss lady now. Seems like she ran out of juice."

So his grandmother had finally run out of steam.

I wonder how much damage she caused?

Colin sniffed the air. There were so many foreign scents in here that it made his head swim, and he couldn't keep a clear picture of his surroundings. The dragon gave off a smoky scent, but the giant creature stank like garbage and reminded him of Gareth Dugan.

Must be a full ogre.

A few of the other inmates had a scent similar to the goth twin's mother.

Vampires.

On that pleasant realization, he caught a familiar

whiff of lavender.

Granny Strauss.

The elevator doors at the far end of the hallway swished open revealing two large guards escorting his tiny grandmother. A distinctly burned smell followed both guards. Colin smiled.

They must have met the wrong end of a lightning bolt.

His grandmother was handcuffed, her clothing looked a little scorched, and her hair stuck out at odd angles. Colin noted that she looked very happy with herself.

Her blind eyes searched the cellblock as she walked until she settled on Colin. "Thought you might get yourself caught up here," said his grandmother.

"Hi, Gran," said Colin, genuinely happy to see her.

Amazing what a difference a week can make.

The elevator doors opened again, and Mr. Emerson walked out. Colin could now easily recognize the smell of his aftershave and—

Aftershave. Scent.

The realization hit Colin so hard he thought he might throw up. He began pacing back and forth, trying to put the pieces together.

"Put her next to the dragon," ordered Mr. Emerson.

Colin was vaguely aware of the guard pushing something on his control panel, and the bars in the empty cell next to the dragon retracted into the ceiling. The old woman shuffled in and turned around to let one of the large guards remove the handcuffs. After her escort exited the cell, the bars slid smoothly back into place.

"Now listen here, Beatrice," began Mr. Emerson. "I

don't know why you suddenly felt the compulsion to help your grandson when you clearly knew what he was or why you put at least ten of my best men in the hospital last night. The fact is, we still need you to maintain the cover over Elkwood, and I need to know we can still trust you to do so."

"Don't you worry about the weather," said Mrs. Strauss, "I'll keep us hidden like I always do."

"I'd like you stay here for a while and cool down. And then we'll talk about getting you back to Elkwood."

"That seems reasonable," said Colin's grandmother.

Colin noted the slight change in his grandmother's heartbeat.

She's lying.

Colin focused back to the task at hand. The werewolf Silas was hunting had been bitten outside of Elkwood and then came back here. Elkwood was too small a town to try to hide in plain sight. But if you're a werewolf and you want to hide it, especially if you know there's another werewolf in town, you'd want to keep yourself hidden by disguising yourself. You'd want to keep your head shaved so no one notices the change in your hair. You'd want to wear something that would throw off the scent of the other creatures in town, the vampires, the werewolves—

Mr. Winter is the other werewolf!

It all made sense. He was out of town all the time. Since he got back from his last trip, he had been sick, and his usual butt-hole-esque behavior had gotten worse. He'd threatened Colin in the bathroom and made jokes about Sam Bale's death. Mr. Winter would also know that there was another werewolf in town because he was in the town hall meeting the night it was interrupted. The same night Silas bit Colin.

And the aftershave! He was using the aftershave to cover his scent so a vampire or werewolf couldn't recognize him! Mr. Winter killed Sam Bale.

He's going to kill Becca!

"You have to let me out!" Colin blurted, his face pressed against the bars. "I know who the werewolf is."

Mr. Emerson turned around. "You're the werewolf. You and your friend there. I know you don't want us to know, but one of you killed that boy."

"It's not true! Mr. Winter is the killer!"

"Mr. Winter? The biology teacher? Don't be ridiculous. He's a member of the town council and a consultant for us. He's been a part of the Elkwood community since the start. Mr. Winter is more than aware of the town's true purpose."

"And he hates it," said Colin, his mind racing. "That's why he leaves on vacation all the time. He must have been bitten while on vacation. Silas said the werewolf had killed someone else and he had tracked it here. Mr. Winter went through the same changes I did. He's acting erratic in class, he's shaved his head to hide the hair growth, and he wears aftershave to cover his scent. The day Sam Bale was killed, he was away sick! You have to believe me."

"Colin Strauss, I have absolutely no reason to believe you. All of this sounds ridiculous. You'd say anything to divert attention away from yourself at this point." Mr. Emerson moved closer to Colin. "The truth is, I don't know what you're capable of. But we're going to find out."

"Your daughter is in danger! Don't you care?"

"Becca is under guard and will go to school like normal, and neither you nor your friend can hurt her."

Colin slammed the bars. He reached for the wolf inside him, but it was still too far away somewhere behind the fog.

"Try and keep that anger in check," threatened Mr. Emerson, "or we'll have to put you down." With that, he turned and walked toward the elevator.

Colin looked over to Silas who was still sleeping and then to his grandmother. An overwhelming sense of helplessness filled his heart.

"Do you know for sure? Are you absolutely certain Winter is the killer?" asked his grandmother.

"You two pipe down," said the guard from his desk.

"I'm certain," said Colin. "It has to be. It makes perfect sense."

"And you can stop him?"

"I have to try."

"Hey! What'd I just say?" called the guard. "I won't hesitate to tranquilize you wolf-kid, and you," said the guard, gesturing to Colin's grandmother, "that sort of insubordination is what got you thrown in here in the first place."

Colin's grandmother gripped the bars of her cell with both hands. Her cloudy eyes staring out toward the guard. "Oh, I didn't get thrown in here."

Colin felt the air in the cellblock change.

"I wanted to be here," said his grandmother.

Electricity shot from her hands and spiralled up the bars of the cell. The control panel in front of the guard began to spark and then exploded, throwing the guard backward. Mr. Emerson turned from the elevator along with the two large guards who had escorted his grandmother. Another shot of electricity flashed across the bars of the old lady's cell and jumped around the room. Colin stepped back from his own bars as lightning struck them.

"No!" shouted Mr. Emerson.

The bars on every cell began to raise slowly, much to the surprise and joy of the inmates.

"Go get him," said Colin's grandmother with a smile.

Colin dived under his bars and stood just as the first large guard reached him.

The guard had at least one hundred pounds on him, but Colin still had his increased strength and sense even if he couldn't fully turn. The guard made to grab him, but Colin ducked under those large arms and drove his fist hard into his stomach. Colin heard the guard's lungs deflate as he gasped to catch his breath and crumpled in a heap. Jumping over the body, Colin met the other guard head on, grabbing the big man's fist and flinging him across the cellblock where he crashed into the wall and slid to the ground.

Other inmates escaped their cells; some were fighting while the ogre was trying to squeeze under his cell bars, getting angrier and angrier.

Turning, Colin came face-to-face with the barrel of Mr. Emerson's gun.

"Sorry, kid." Mr. Emerson fired, and time slowed down.

Colin could hear the chaos of the cellblock, the

creature's angry shouts, and his grandmother's maniacal laughter as lightning zapped around the cells. The tranquilizer dart exited the gun, and he knew that he could dodge it. He shifted his weight and jumped high into the air, over the dart, over Mr. Emerson, and landed lightly. Colin turned, grabbed the key card clipped to Mr. Emerson's belt, and punched the man square in the jaw. Mr. Emerson folded to the ground.

Colin hated that it felt so good. After all, he just knocked out his new girlfriend's dad. Not the best way to win him over.

***

Alarms sounded from every direction making Colin's head ring as he ascended in the elevator. He'd had to tackle seventeen more guards on several different floors as the elevator had stopped a few times already.

The doors slid open at the main floor, and Colin stepped into the hangar and ran for the exit. He burst out into the early-morning air to find it was raining. It felt good to be outside.

Again, he reached for the wolf and tried to bring on the change, but it wouldn't happen. The power was still out of his reach.

He didn't know how he was going to stop Mr. Winter, but he had to try. He had to save Becca.

A dark-green army truck swung into the yard and skidded to a stop. Men began to file out of the back, and

Colin didn't waste any more time. He ran across the yard, picking up speed until he was close to the fence, and jumped, clearing the razor wire and the cliff ledge and plummeted toward the ground. He landed heavily but didn't miss a step. Adrenaline surged through him, and it felt good to be running again, even if it was in human form. He followed his own scent back toward Elkwood.

Chapter Nineteen

Dogfight

Colin didn't know what he was going to do. He didn't have a plan besides hoping he was right that Mr. Winter was the other werewolf.

A deer darted out of his way as Colin raced on through the forest, resisting the urge to chase it. A pang of emptiness hit him as he crossed the stream where he had first changed. He reached for the wolf inside, but the change wouldn't come. Anger made him run faster.

It wouldn't take the goon squad back at the base long to get themselves together and come for him. For all Colin knew, they were already on their way to Elkwood. Colin had to get to the school, find Becca, and make sure she was okay, and then … what? Go up to his biology teacher and accuse him of being a werewolf? How would he ever prove it? Once Mr. Emerson and his small army showed up, it'd all be over.

Colin felt a small stab of regret at having punched Mr. Emerson, but the thought was fleeting. After all, the man had imprisoned him, shot at him, and locked up his grandmother.

Colin wondered how his grandmother was fairing. Knowing what he now did about the little old lady, he immediately followed that thought up with one of extreme pity for all the men, creatures, and dragons locked up with her.

As Colin neared Elkwood School, the scent in the air changed from damp forest to the smell of cut grass on the football field and an ungodly odor emanating from the school cafeteria. Moments later, he emerged from the forest and stood at the edge of the football field.

Colin's heart was beating fast from the run, but he wasn't tired. If anything, he felt invigorated. His inner wolf was getting restless, but he still couldn't reach the creature through the fog. He was going to have to go this alone.

His necromancer girlfriend was in trouble. Colin wasn't sure how the shining armor was going to fit, but he couldn't just let her be killed. He finally had an honest shot at going on a date. With a girl! No demons, no homicidal werewolf biology teachers, no dragons, no secret government organizations, and no vampires were going to stand in his way.

Colin marched across the football field.

As he reached the back double doors of the school, he heard the bell ring twice to signal the start of the first period. The ringing resonated through his wolf hearing, and his head spun a little.

Colin's first priority was to find Becca; luckily he knew exactly which class she'd be in right now. Thinking he also needed to avoid Principal Hebert when he suddenly remembered who the large ex-marine-looking teacher really was. Principal Hebert was a captain in Commander Emerson's little government army.

Crap.

If Hebert was here, then he'd no doubt already been notified about Colin's escape and—

"Mr. Strauss!" said the booming voice of Principal Hebert.

Colin had been so focused on finding Becca he'd ignored his surroundings again. He turned to his left and laid eyes upon the imposing-looking man.

Hebert had removed his usual jacket and tie and had rolled up his shirtsleeves to show muscular forearms that looked like they could bench-press any number of very heavy things. Colin could hear the man's steady heartbeat but could also smell his fear. Hebert wasn't sure what to make of his adversary after watching Colin change last night. Maybe that would give Colin an edge.

It certainly made sense with so many supernatural children in the school to have a caretaker for them all. That was Principal Hebert's real role here.

"I'm sorry, Colin, but you're going to have to come with me."

"That's not going to happen." Colin had never been more certain of anything before in his life. He had to get into that school and rescue Becca. Chances are Mr. Winter had already heard or smelled him. Colin was running out of time.

Principal Hebert pulled a small, rectangular black box from his left pocket. "This is going to hurt, Colin. And I'm sorry." He slipped his right hand behind his back, unsheathed a long, shiny hunting knife, and held it up. "Silver. We heard from one of our other offices that it's the one thing you creatures can't heal from."

"It should be me who apologizes to you, Principal Hebert."

"For what?"

"I just wanted to say sorry before we get started," said Colin. "You're a good man, and you don't deserve what I'm about to do to you."

The scent of fear coming from Principal Hebert grew stronger. He held up the black box and pressed a button on the side. A bright blue spark appeared at the end of the box. "Do you know what this is?"

"It's a Taser," said Colin.

"This isn't just any Taser. This was developed by our R&D department to take down large creatures. This thing packs a shock that would knock an elephant out."

"I can smell your fear, Hebert. And I can hear your heartbeat. I know you're a trained soldier and you're keeping yourself calm, but I know you're scared. You don't know what I'm capable of, and maybe that makes two of us. I don't fully understand my powers yet. What I do know is that there's another werewolf in your school. And I have to stop him before he kills anyone else."

"I was told you would say that. It doesn't have to be this way, Colin."

Before Colin could respond, Hebert dived and jabbed the Taser at Colin who caught Hebert's wrist in one hand

and grabbed him by the neck with the other. Hebert's fear skyrocketed, his eyes growing wide. His fear was all Colin could smell, and he loved it. He wanted to hunt in that moment, craved the thrill to hunt down and devour prey. He wanted to turn into the wolf. It felt closer but still out of reach. Adrenaline surged through him, and he knew he could end this man's life with a twist of his hand.

But this wasn't his prey.

Hebert raised the silver knife in his right hand. In one swift motion, Colin released the large man, snatched the Taser, and jabbed it at the principal's chest. Hebert wasn't lying about the power of the device. It threw the former-Marine back several feet where he crumpled in a disorganized heap; the silver knife skittered across the concrete. Colin crushed the Taser device in one hand and dropped it. He pushed open the doors and entered the school.

The smell of aftershave hit him, and Colin's anger burned inside him.

He must be bathing in the stuff.

Hello, Colin.

It was Mr. Winter's voice in Colin's head.

You're late for class.

I'll be there soon.

I'll be waiting.

Colin crossed the hallway and pushed open the double doors to the gym. The fastest way to the biology classroom was to cut across the gymnasium. The large room was empty except for Jeremy who was shooting hoops.

"Colin!" said Jeremy. "Where have you been? You're getting later and later all the time."

"What are you doing here, Jer? Shouldn't you be in class?"

"Shouldn't you?"

"Fair point. I've had a rough night."

"Tell me about it. I ate an entire box of Pop-Tarts before bed. Tossed and turned all night."

Poor Jeremy. I wonder what he really is?

"So why aren't you in class?" said Colin.

Jeremy shot from the three-point line. Nothing but net. "Winter cancelled class today. Said he was too busy with something and that we were all inconsequential in the grand scheme of things. That's a direct quote."

"That's it? He just sent everyone away for a spare period?"

"Yup, figured I'd get some extra b-ball practice in. I think Becca stayed behind though. Hey! Rumor has it you two hooked up or something? Way to go, Col!"

"Becca stayed behind? Why?"

"Winter said he wanted to talk to her about a special project or something. So did you kiss her yet?"

"I gotta go, Jer." Colin started heading for the doors at the opposite end of the gym.

"All right. Don't tell me. See if I care." Jeremy shot again. *Swish.*

Colin reached the doors, then stopped, and turned back to Jeremy. "Jeremy, do you know about Elkwood?"

"What do you mean?"

"Elkwood. The town meetings, the vampires, the witches, the demons?"

Jeremy laughed. "Too many late night movies there, Col? You need to get more sleep, buddy."

Smiling, Colin nodded, then pushed his way through the doors. Jeremy was as oblivious as ever and apparently had no idea who or what he was. Colin wondered how many more people were unaware to what Elkwood really was.

Colin ran down the hallway toward the biology classroom. The smell of aftershave was getting stronger. He could hear Mr. Winter's voice through the door. He was talking about predators.

"In the animal kingdom," said Mr. Winter, "a hierarchy is often established with the alpha predators of the world dominating and ultimately eradicating the lesser of the species."

A few students walked down the hallway, but other than that, it was empty. Most people would still be in class while the biology students would be busy taking full advantage of the spare period.

This was crazy.

I don't even know the extent or the limits of my powers.

But if he didn't do something, more people would die. Becca would die. That wasn't something he was willing to accept. Silas said he could heal from almost any wound except silver. He still had his strength, his speed, his other gifts.

Colin closed his eyes and tried to focus, to trust his senses. He could hear the general hum of the school. Teachers droning on. The placid rhythm of student's heartbeats. The smell of bad food being prepped in the kitchen.

He pushed his hearing in on the biology classroom, and he could see the room clearly in his mind. Scents and sounds mixing to paint the perfect picture.

Mr. Winter was still talking, his heartbeat racing. Colin could smell his excitement and anticipation. There was a second heartbeat in the room, also racing. A familiar scent also greeted him despite the strong stench of fear and anger surrounding it.

Colin opened his eyes, kicked open the door, and entered the classroom.

Mr. Winter sat smirking with his feet up on his desk. Aftershave burned Colin's nostrils. He could only imagine how bad it must be for the biology teacher. Mr. Winter's hair had grown since last night.

Tied to a chair in the middle of the room, Becca sat gagged with tears streaking down her face. She looked exhausted and afraid, but Colin could smell her relief when she saw him.

"Mr. Strauss. So nice of you to join us. Don't think about freeing our resident teenage witch just yet. We have some talking to do first."

"I don't think there's much to talk about," said Colin.

"Oh, but I think there is. Do you know what a rare species we are these days? Werewolves. I think it'd be educational for us to swap our origin stories. We are in a school after all."

"I was bitten a few days ago by a werewolf who came here looking to kill you." Colin didn't see the point in hiding it.

Mr. Winter swung his legs down off his desk. "That's right! The hunter," said Mr. Winter. "The wolf that bit me was part of a group looking to take over the world. They keep turning people into werewolves in the hope of spreading their bloodline and growing the pack, but this hunter of yours keeps killing them. He seems very motivated."

"I think he just likes the world the way it is."

Mr. Winter slammed his fists down on his desk, splintering and denting the wood. "That's not his choice to make!"

Colin could hear Mr. Winter's uneven heartbeat. The biology teacher was having trouble keeping his change at bay, and his erratic emotions weren't helping anything.

Colin reached for his own wolf, but it was still hidden somewhere. He thought he could hear it growling in his head. "Why are you doing this? Why kill Sam or anyone for that matter?"

Mr. Winter laughed. "Do you know what it's like to be a schoolteacher? Or even worse, a schoolteacher in a town full of freaks? It's unbearable. All you snivelling little beasts, showing up late, never doing your homework. Ungrateful little whelps. Half of them powerful beings and taking everything for granted! Whining about this and that. Pitiful!"

Colin took a small quick sidestep toward Becca. "Must be annoying for you."

"It's infuriating. I found that taking the occasional vacation, swimming in a hot climate, getting a massage on the beach, was all I ever needed to lead a calm, fulfilling life. Of course, then I come back here, and it all starts over again."

"But on the last trip you were bitten."

"I was, and then the changes started. By the time I came back to Elkwood, I'd already gone through my first change. You know what it feels like. It's amazing! The raw power! It makes you realize how truly insignificant every single other person on the planet really is."

"I wouldn't totally agree with you there."

Just need to keep him talking. Keep him distracted.

Colin took another quick step closer to Becca.

"That Bale boy had it coming. Do you know he never turned in a homework assignment? Not once. Never. Two years in my class and not one shred of homework."

"So it was you who killed Sam Bale?"

Another step. He was within eight feet of her.

"When your friend disrupted the town hall meeting the other night, I went on a little hunt of my own. I didn't just kill Mr. Bale. I ate him! He was delicious."

"And now—"

"And now I'm going to eat your little girlfriend here. I could smell you all over her as soon as she walked into the class this morning. After last night's town hall meeting, I think it's high time I left Elkwood for good. There's nothing here for me anyway."

"Surely that's not true," said Colin. "Didn't you mention having a cat once?"

"I ate it."

Another step.

"Poor cat."

"I'll eat her and then you and then I'll be on my way. I might even take out a few more students on my way out. As a parting gift. To me. Good-bye, Mr. Strauss."

Colin could feel the tension in the room shift. Mr.

Winter's heart began to beat wildly. It was all familiar to Colin; this is what happened before the change started. It felt like your heart was going to explode and then—

Mr. Winter picked up the edge of the desk with one hand and threw it aside. It crashed against the far window. Glass smashed, and the desk broke into pieces.

The biology teacher ripped open his shirt as the change ran through his body.

Colin hadn't seen it from this point of view before. It was almost elegant. Mr. Winter's body increased in size while black hair shot out all over. Muscles expanded and tightened. His ears grew to points, and his jaw jutted into a snout. Claws grew from his hands and toes as the remainder of his clothing fell, shredded during transformation. It was over in moments. Mr. Winter's ears brushed the ceiling, and his large frame was almost the same width as the whiteboard behind him. He dropped to all fours, planting his massive clawed hands on the ground, and let out a growl.

Your move, Mr. Strauss.

Colin didn't know what move to make exactly. He'd only really had one plan, and that was to keep Mr. Winter talking long enough for him to get closer to Becca. He really hadn't fully thought it all through.

Mr. Winter charged toward them, claws ripping into the floor. Colin spun and shoved Becca's chair to the back of the class.

Colin turned back in time for Mr. Winter to tackle him. The impact knocked the air out of Colin's lungs, but he hung on to Mr. Winter's head and swung himself onto his back, grabbing the creature's ears.

Mr. Winter flailed wildly, jaws snapping, trying to dislodge Colin who was holding on for dear life. The giant wolf flipped his head forward, and Colin somersaulted over the top and landed lightly on the ground. He grabbed a nearby chair and swung it with all his might, but Mr. Winter was too fast in his wolf form. He knocked the chair aside and picked Colin up by the throat with one massive, hairy hand.

Colin could feel the creature's claws tearing his skin. Mr. Winter growled and threw Colin through the air with such force that he crashed straight through the wall and across the hallway, slamming into the lockers on the other side.

Covered in drywall dust, Colin was grateful for the pain that refused to let him pass out. His ribs were certainly broken, along with his left arm, which sat at an awkward angle across his leg. When he crashed through the wall, his right leg had snagged on some metal framing, and his thigh had been opened in a bloody red gash. Colin's skin began to tingle around his injuries as heat flooded his body.

The gash on his leg began to knit together. First, the torn muscle inside, then the skin moved back together, and a moment later, the injury was gone. He moved his left arm, and the bone cracked back into place. He felt his ribs pop back into alignment, the tingly heat sensation subsiding as all the nicks and cuts on his body disappeared.

Colin stood up and steadied himself against the locker as Mr. Winter forcefully pushed into the hallway through the Colin-shaped hole in wall.

Students were crowding into the corridor to see what all the noise was about. They all watched as the giant snarling creature that had just thrown a student through a wall stood to his full height.

Colin had to get the students out of the school. He looked around for a solution, and then he found it. A fire alarm. He pulled down on the red switch, and an alarm screamed through the halls. Students ran in the opposite direction of the werewolf.

Mr. Winter let out a throaty growl that could easily have been a laugh.

Colin faced the creature again. Mr. Winter had at least three feet on him.

One of the outside doors was kicked open, and Principal Hebert stepped into the building. He was holding the silver knife, and he looked angry. Until he saw the werewolf.

Mr. Winter dropped to all fours and raced at the principal who stood his ground, out of either heroism, fear, or just plain confusion. Hebert tried to swing the blade upward, but he wasn't fast enough. Mr. Winter sunk his jaws into the large man's shoulder and shook him like a ragdoll before flinging him into a wall. The blade clattered to the floor as the werewolf loomed over the battered body of Principal Hebert.

"No!" shouted Colin. But it was too late. Mr. Winter clamped his jaws down on the principal's throat with a sickening crunch. Colin heard the final beats of the principal's heart as the life rushed out of him.

Colin jumped through the hole in the wall and ran to untie Becca as quickly as possible.

"Where is he?" asked Becca after Colin pulled the gag off her. She was pale and shaken, but there was an air of determination about her.

"He's in the hallway, eating Principal Hebert."

"Oh no." Tears welled up in her eyes.

"It's okay. It'll be okay."

"How do you know that? Can't you do something? Can't you change?"

"I can't. Your dad injected me with something to stop me from changing."

Colin could hear movement in the hallway. Mr. Winter was done with his kill.

"We have to go," said Colin, "now!"

Becca and Colin climbed through the hole in time to see Mr. Winter pick up the knife. He held it in one massive hand and touched a clawed finger to the blade. Colin could see and smell his skin burning.

"Interesting," said Mr. Winter slowly. Apparently he'd also discovered he could speak while in werewolf form. "Colliinn," growled Mr. Winter menacingly.

"Run," said Colin to Becca.

"What about you?"

"I'll be fine, go!"

"Are you sure?"

Colin gave her a gentle shove and turned back to face the werewolf. Blood visible in his teeth, Mr. Winter stank of death.

I'm going to hurt you, Mr. Strauss.

"Can't we wait until after lunch? I'm a little hungry," said Colin. Part of him actually meant it. He hadn't eaten since yesterday, and he was starving. Colin backed up as

Mr. Winter slowly stalked toward him.

I already ate.

"Right," said Colin glancing at the silver knife.

Don't worry about the knife. I'll save it for the end.

The realization hit Colin hard. Through the stench of death and aftershave, Colin could smell happiness. It wasn't just happiness; it was sheer joy. Mr. Winter was enjoying this. He wasn't going to kill Colin yet. He was going to have fun with his prey first.

Colin had taken plenty of beatings before. Gareth Dugan had laid him out flat more times than he could remember. However, Gareth was a bully because he wanted people to be afraid of him. Mr. Winter was a different case. He was the worst kind of bully. He bullied because he really enjoyed it. Colin stopped backing away and prepared himself for the beating of a lifetime.

***

Several minutes later, Colin crashed through the front doors of the school; wood splintering everywhere, as he cleared the steps, and rolled to a stop in the parking lot.

There was an audible gasp and a few screams from the students and teachers in the parking lot as Colin lay still.

Colin wasn't dead, though it didn't seem like a bad option. Mr. Winter had beaten and thrown Colin around the school. He'd been broken and cut, his body healing itself as quickly as possible. Beaten again and again, Colin's body would keep knitting itself back together, muscles reconnecting, and broken bones clicking back into place.

Colin rolled onto his back and took inventory of his injuries.

Fractured skull, broken arm and leg this time, claw marks across my back and face, and I think that my spine is in two pieces. Maybe three.

Once again, his body started to put itself back together. The fixing was almost as painful as the actual injury. His whole body was slowly going numb.

Maybe if I lie here, he'll just leave me alone.

There was a blood-curdling howl from inside the school.

Probably not.

Colin sat up and looked over to his right where two hundred pairs of eyes stared back at him with a mixture of shock, surprise, and fear. Colin gave them a small wave. He noticed Becca standing among the group; she moved to him, but he held up a hand and shook his head.

Colin?

Silas? Is that really you?

It's me. Where are you?

I'm at the school. Mr. Winter is the other werewolf!

The aftershave guy?

Yes! He's here, in wolf form.

Are you okay?

Not really. He's been kinda beating the crap out of me. I think he's going to kill me.

I'm on my way. The inhibitor they gave us, the injection, it wears off. I'll be there soon. Try and keep him busy!

Yeah, I'll just let him pummel me for another ten minutes.

Colin got to his feet and reached out for his wolf but failed to make contact.

He tried again.

Nothing.

Crap.

Mr. Winter leaped from the school entrance and landed a few feet from Colin on all fours, the silver knife still clutched in his hand.

The crowd stepped back a few feet, and several people ran away screaming.

With all the freaks and creatures in this town, you'd think they'd be less scared.

You're right, Colin. They should be more afraid. Allow me to educate them.

Mr. Winter turned toward the crowd, stood up on two legs, and roared.

The scent of fear was strong.

"No!" said Becca, standing at the front of the crowd. "You won't hurt anyone else!"

Mr. Winter growled ferociously.

Colin's senses picked up the pheromones pouring off the large beast, signaling his intent. Mr. Winter had given off the same smell before he killed Principal Hebert. Colin had also encountered it at the crime scene the night he sneaked out with Becca. It was the scent of pure evil.

Mr. Winter was going to kill Becca.

He's going to kill my girlfriend.

The realization broke something inside him.

A primal, guttural growl tore from deep within Colin's throat. Mr. Winter stopped in his tracks.

The serum was wearing off, Colin could feel it. Like a wall tumbling down, power tingled through his body. He could feel his wolf again, and it was not happy. His words came out deep and unearthly. "Get. Away. From. My. Girlfriend."

The change surged through him like a tidal wave. It was the fastest he'd ever shifted. His muscles and hair exploded outward, teeth elongated, claws flicked out, his clothes shredded as he quickly increased in size.

Mr. Winter turned slowly.

Colin hadn't realized how big he was as a werewolf. He even towered over Mr. Winter.

"Finally," said Mr. Winter.

Colin dived at the biology teacher, claws at the ready, teeth bared in a snarl.

They collided hard, jaws snapping, claws tearing through hair and flesh.

Colin heard a car screech to a stop and the smell of Mr. Emerson wafted through the air.

Grabbing Mr. Winter's throat, Colin lifted him from the ground. Mr. Winter struggled, kicking out, but missing the mark. Colin slammed him into the ground, cracking the concrete. Lifted him back up and did it again and again and again and again. Mr. Winter's body went limp, but Colin couldn't stop. He just kept driving him into the ground.

In that moment, Colin felt more wolf than human, and he wanted nothing more than to tear the evil creature in two.

"Colin, no!" Becca's voice. "You're better than him."

Colin released the giant creature, and it thudded to the ground. He turned and looked at Becca who was only a few feet away now. Colin was slightly ashamed that part of him still wanted to kill Mr. Winter. For Sam Bale. For Principal Hebert. And for whomever else had died at the hands of this monster. But Becca wanted him to stop, and he couldn't ignore her. She was his voice of reason.

She smiled, the one that he loved, but it vanished quickly and turned to fear. "Colin! Behind you!"

The warning reached him too late. The knife sunk deep into Colin's left shoulder, and he cried out in pain as the blade dragged down his back. The blade was ice cold but the blood quickly covering his back was burning hot.

The past week spun through his mind as he began to feel dizzy. Anger boiled up from deep inside, giving him a moment of clarity. He spun around and grabbed Mr. Winter's head with his left hand, ignoring the pain shooting through his body, and sunk his right-hand claws deep into the large wolf creature's side, clamping his jaws down hard and deep into his enemy's shoulder.

Mr. Winter let out a cry. Colin's vision blurred, his pounding blood a drumbeat drowning out all other sound. Caught in a frenzy, Colin was unable to stop himself as he dug deeper. His senses focused in on the object of his desire; all he could see and smell was red.

He could hear Becca screaming, Mr. Emerson shouting orders, students crying. He could even sense Silas nearby. But he couldn't stop. This monster deserved to die.

Colin clamped his teeth around the barely beating heart of Mr. Winter and swallowed it whole.

It tasted better than deer.

Exhaustion overcame him. He staggered backward and collapsed heavily onto the concrete. His breath was coming in ragged gasps, and he could feel his own blood pooling beneath him. It felt warm and sticky, and he wondered how he would ever be able to wash it out of his hair.

He could vaguely make out the shape of Becca screaming something as her dad tried to restrain her.

Strong girl.

I'm sorry, Colin.

Silas. I think I'm dying.

And then Becca was there, kneeling over him. She was talking, but he couldn't hear her. His senses were failing. She closed her eyes and placed both hands on his chest. Becca's hands felt warm, and that warmth spread throughout his body like someone pouring warm honey through his veins. It felt comfortable and safe, and Colin felt that dying with this feeling wouldn't be the worst thing in the world. It was peaceful.

Ever so slowly, the world turned to black as Colin Strauss, Elkwood's first teenage werewolf, died.

Epilogue

One Month Later

Wake up!

Colin's eyes snapped open. It was still dark, but that didn't matter. He uncurled himself from his sleeping spot at the end of his bed and stretched.

What do you want, Silas?

Training session. Forest. Ten minutes.

Can't we have midday training sessions? These early-morning ones get in the way of my beauty sleep.

Nine minutes.

I'll be there.

Colin stood slowly and stretched again. The now familiar pain shot across the scar on his left shoulder blade. He looked at it in the mirror. It had healed fairly well, but the scar was long and jagged, running diagonally from his left shoulder down to the middle of his spine.

Colin had been unconscious for almost forty-eight

hours after the fight with Mr. Winter. According to Silas, after Colin stopped breathing, Becca had knelt unmoving for six hours as she tried to bring him back to life and heal his wounds. Apparently, Mr. Emerson had tried to pull her off several times, but she refused to give up.

The first thing Colin remembered was waking up in a bed at the army base surrounded by heavily armed guards. Becca didn't wake up for another day or two. Bringing Colin back from the dead had been her first full resurrection, and it had taken a lot out of her.

Colin pulled on a pair of sweatpants and a hoodie. There was no point in dressing warmly as Silas would want him to change anyway. He'd already ruined three T-shirts and two pairs of jeans through sudden changes over the last couple of weeks. Colin moved quickly and quietly down the stairs.

"Where are you off to so early?" said his grandmother, already parked in front of the TV, a cup of steaming coffee in her hand.

"Training session with Silas."

"You should eat something first," she said. "There's leftover steak in the fridge."

Colin knew this; he could smell it.

"Thanks, Gran." He headed into the kitchen, took the plate of steak out of the fridge, and devoured it in under a minute. "Bye, Gran," said Colin as he headed out the door.

"Don't be out too long. You'll be late for school," she shouted after him.

"Yes, Gran."

"I'll make sure the rain holds off until you're done."

"Thanks, Gran."

Colin closed the door, jumped from the porch to the sidewalk, and started his jog toward the edge of the forest.

The relationship with his grandmother had vastly improved over the last month. She was still the same cranky old lady, but there were no secrets between them. His grandmother no longer had to hide that she was a witch, and she even seemed to like the fact that Colin wasn't just some ordinary kid. They now ate dinner together almost every night and held conversations that weren't centered around Colin being a useless idiot.

Mr. Emerson had tried several times to detain her, but eventually some sort of order had come down from a higher authority that told him to leave her alone. Since the deranged old witch was essential to the security and, thanks to her control over the weather, invisibility of Elkwood, she was allowed to go crazy and injure several people from time to time.

Colin reached the edge of the forest as the sun began to rise. He could smell Silas nearby. These early morning training sessions were a mandatory requirement of Elkwood's newly reformed government.

After the event at the school, Silas and Colin had undergone several days of interrogations and medical tests. A review board was sent in to determine the threat level of the Elkwood werewolves and whether they should be allowed to live. None of it concerned Colin too much since he was still taking some heavy medicine to help him deal with the pain. Some guy named Commander Elrick Varson finally sat down with the two of them in a small metal room to deliver their sentence.

"Gentlemen, it's been a pleasure to work with you both this week," began Varson.

"Get to the point," interrupted Silas who was sick to death of being poked, prodded, and asked questions.

Varson adjusted his tie. It struck Colin as a nervous reaction because his heartbeat increased slightly every time he did it. "In light of recent events, I'll be joining the Elkwood community as the new commander of this district. We're dropping all charges against you, including the prison break, resisting arrest, and the murder and consumption of Mr. Winter. In our eyes, you did us and this town a service. As long as you don't make a habit of eating people, I think we'll all be okay."

Colin nodded in agreement as Varson continued. "As I'm sure you've figured out by now, Elkwood isn't our only district that holds people, well, creatures ... uh, class five is how we refer to your kind or kinds."

Tie readjusted to the left.

"But we consider Elkwood to be one of our most important towns as it was the first one of its kind. Commander Emerson will be staying on as my second in command and will be heading up a new division here."

"Is this you getting to the point?" said Silas. "We've been stuck with needles, interrogated, and held here for five days. I don't care about some stinking new division that—"

"Ah!" said Varson. "That's exactly where you're wrong."

Tie adjusted farther to the left so it actually looked a little stupid now.

"The information that Colin provided us in regards

to Mr. Winter and the group of werewolves who are turning people with the purpose of building some sort of an army was troubling to say the least. We currently have a similar problem with vampires in Eastern Europe. Not to mention the demons who are trying to take over Los Angeles by infiltrating the movie business. It's just a mess. Towns like Elkwood were founded to keep class fives safe and to monitor them so, if there was ever a need, we could mobilize them."

Silas laughed.

"Am I missing the joke?" said Colin.

"It's no joke," said Varson. "We want you both to work with us. The new division under Commander Emerson has been codenamed 'Night Watch.' Consisting of small teams of class fives who will operate out of Elkwood, it will help us deal with class five problems throughout the world. You, Silas, would be our first recruit, and your first order of business would be to train Colin."

Silas wasn't laughing anymore.

You're not laughing. Are you considering this?

I don't know. I've travelled the world for a long time. Lived under rocks, as you say. It wouldn't be the worst thing to have a home. I could watch that Gromlin movie.

Gremlins.

And if this is real and not just a way to tag and leash us, then I'd have the resources to keep tracking down these other werewolves.

"Are you guys doing that mind thing?" said Varson, adjusting his tie back to the center. "I find that fascinating."

Varson truly did seem fascinated by them. Colin sensed

a certain amount of jealousy, maybe even wolf-envy.

After hammering out a few details, the three ultimately agreed on terms and became the first members of Night Watch. Silas wanted a steady wage as he hadn't had one since the Dark Ages. He also wanted free range of the forests surrounding Elkwood for training and hunting purposes, which was why Colin stood at the edge of the tree line naked.

Silas loomed out of the shadows, already changed into his wolf form.

You're late.

"You know my grandmother. She made me eat a steak before leaving the house. I think she's still worried I'm going to eat someone."

Do you ever feel the urge to?

"What? No. Wait, do you?"

No. Well. Sometimes.

"That's gross."

Says the boy who ate his biology teacher.

It had been a great source of pride and amusement for Silas that Colin had been the one to take down Mr. Winter even though it almost cost Colin his life.

C'mon, change already. I don't want you to be late for school again.

Colin changed with ease. It still hurt, but he could shift even faster than Silas now. Before he'd fully finished changing, Silas took off into the forest, which meant they were going to hunt each other. Colin followed the older wolf's scent.

For three weeks they had trained most mornings and some nights too. Night Watch wouldn't begin official operation until the new year, so they still had a few months to prepare. Even then, it was unlikely that Colin would be allowed to go out on any missions immediately. He was only thirteen after all.

Silas had taught Colin a lot about his wolf side, and despite being a bit rough around the edges, Silas was turning out to be a great teacher.

It wasn't easy, but Colin was getting better. He'd already mastered partial changes so he could access more of his wolf strength without going through a full change. He could partially change his hands and face quite easily.

While undergoing tests at the army base, the scientists had made the discovery that every human had a werewolf gene inside them. They concluded that the gene was likely more common in the past but had grown increasingly recessive. A werewolf bite activated that gene and triggered the change. The more prominent the gene, the stronger the werewolf. Colin's unusual, early change indicated that his gene was exceptionally strong, explaining why he changed so quickly and why he picked everything up so fast.

Silas's scent had grown cold which meant he'd taken to the trees, but Colin was getting better and better at anticipating the old dog's tricks. Trusting his senses, Colin dropped to all fours and closed his eyes. The forest was alive with activity: animals waking up or going to sleep, water trickling from the nearby stream, leaves in the trees rustling, an electric energy indicating rain wasn't far away. To his left he could hear steady breathing. Colin opened his eyes, stood, and in one swift movement, climbed the tree to his left. About halfway up, he leaped toward the dark shape perched on a thick branch.

The two werewolves collided and fell back to the ground, both landing lightly.

How did you possibly know I was there?

You breathe heavily after running.

Let's see how you breathe when you're a few hundred years old.

Whatever you say, old man.

Silas swatted him with a big paw playfully. **You'd better go, kid. You're going to be late.**

Colin took off at a run, quickly outpacing Silas, who fell behind probably to hunt some poor unsuspecting animal.

Colin changed back to human form at the edge of the forest and pulled on his clothes. He'd already stashed his school bag in his locker, so he didn't need to go home, and he'd just shower later. He barely ever broke a sweat these days so body odor wasn't a problem.

Shaving was probably his biggest issue as his hair growth was rapid. He already had stubble this morning, and that was after shaving late last night. The hair on his head had grown thick and unruly, and the muscles on his body had continued to grow gradually. Fortunately, he liked his clothing baggy, so he hadn't grown out of anything yet, but it was definitely getting tighter.

Colin reached the front school gates and paused for a moment by the flowers in honor of Principal Hebert. The community still mourned his loss, and those who knew his true function, which turned out to be most of Elkwood, had raised concerns about who would be the new caretaker of the school. As of yet, no one had been appointed, but apparently someone was on their way from another community and would be taking over soon. In the meantime, Varson had appointed guards to the school. The normal kids at the school who had no idea what Elkwood really was, were told they were stepping up security after the murder of their principal. "The Norms," as Elkwood residents called them, has been magically glamoured to believe they hadn't seen their biology teacher and classmate turn into giant werewolves, fight in front of the school, and that they absolutely had not seen one of them eat the other one.

"Colin!"

I love her voice.

Becca ran over to meet Colin, and they kissed. Because they could. Much to the anger, frustration, and disapproval of Mr. Emerson. Colin could smell his displeasure as he watched from the driver's seat of his car. Colin gave him a small wave and nodded politely. "Do you think your dad is ever going to like me?"

"Well, you did hurt a lot of his men."

"True."

"You did knock him out."

"He was going to shoot me!"

"Don't worry. I still like you."

"That's all that really matters."

They kissed again. Because they could.

"Enough, please, yuck, gross, and just no!" said Jeremy jokingly as he joined them.

"Morning, Jer," said Colin.

The three of them headed into the school where people either greeted Colin or avoided him like the plague because they were mentally and emotionally scarred by what he was.

It didn't matter to Colin. In fact, he was more popular now than he'd ever been. Turns out that he had cracked the formula for turning from zero to hero in the eyes of middle-school students: you just have to eat the teacher everyone hates the most.

The school day passed quickly. Class schedules had been rewritten so the goth twins and Colin never had class together. Much to Becca's relief, Tori had also been removed from Colin's class schedule as her abilities as a siren played havoc with his senses. Gareth Dugan had also requested a class switch, afraid Colin would inflict some sort of terrible revenge on the bully who had made his life miserable for over a year. Colin didn't intend on doing anything of the sort, but it gave him a certain amount of pleasure that Gareth was terrified of him.

Becca and Colin said good-bye at the school gate and agreed to meet up later for a movie night at Jeremy's house. Being a powerful werewolf did wonders for Colin's self-confidence; no longer an introvert, he'd become far more social. It also helped to date the cool, creepy redheaded chick at school.

As he walked home, he pondered everything that had happened. Yes, he'd killed someone. But it was a bad someone, so that's okay, right? Colin had asked Silas how the change would affect his life, worried it was the werewolf that now made him who he was, and if that was the case, was he still himself? Silas had a simple answer, as he always seemed to.

"You're worried how it'll change you as a person?"

said Silas. "That's easy. It doesn't. Whatever you are inside, whoever you were before I bit you and turned you into a werewolf, that's still who you are today. You always had the potential to be whatever you wanted to be. Everyone does. Whether you step up and make the decision to use that potential, well, that's the difference. That's what makes you who you are. It's you making the choice to be something!"

The rain was falling heavily by the time Colin got home, and he decided to have a shave and a quick shower before dinner. As he dried off and looked at himself in the mirror, Colin realized that Silas was right. He could still see the same person in the reflection. Sure, he had more hair and yes he had muscles now, and his eyes had that crazy amber-colored tint to them. But he was still the same person.

This year he'd stolen a car, been bitten by a giant wolf, turned into a werewolf, eaten his biology teacher, and been drafted into a secret government organization.

This is my life as a teenage werewolf.

He wiped a hand across the mirror to clear the condensation. "Not a loser," said Colin.

His reflection agreed.

THE END
(until the next full moon)

Acknowledgements

When I was young, my Dad used to record movies that were on late at night past my bedtime so I could watch them the next day. Movies like *Abbott and Costello Meet the Wolfman* and *An American Werewolf in London* birthed an interest in the popular hairy creature of the night and twenty five-ish years later, I finally wrote the result of that interest, this novel. With that in mind I need to thank my Dad for filling countless VHS tapes with movies and my Mum for allowing me to watch them (even though such viewing led me to the terrifying belief that there were gremlins living under my bed from age 7-10).

Particular thanks to my agent Mark Gottlieb at the Trident Media Group for his guidance and for believing in my work and helping me shape the tone and voice of the novel. Special thanks to Georgia McBride, Tara Creel, and the team at Month9Books and Tantrum books for their dedication, commitment, and hard work in making this novel the best it can be.

Finally, special thanks to my family for their constant love and support, to my wife Nadia who encourages and inspires me every day, and to my own adorable werewolf-pups, Ashlynn, Gabriel, and Kaidan.

Andrew Buckley

Andrew Buckley attended the Vancouver Film School's Writing for Film and Television program. After pitching and developing several screenplay projects for film and television, he worked in marketing and public relations, before becoming a professional copy and content writer. During this time Andrew began writing his first adult novel, *Death, the Devil and the Goldfish*, followed closely by his second novel, *Stiltskin*. He also writes a spy thriller series under the pen name "Jane D Everly."

Andrew also co-hosts a geek movie podcast, is working on several new novels, and has a stunning amount of other ideas. He now lives happily in the Okanagan Valley, BC with three kids, one cat, one needy dog, one beautiful wife, and a multitude of characters that live comfortably inside of his mind.

Andrew is represented by Mark Gottlieb at the Trident Media Group. www.andrewbuckleyauthor.com

OTHER MONTH9BOOKS TITLES YOU MIGHT LIKE

THE UNDERTAKERS: END OF THE WORLD
DEAD JED: ADVENTURES OF A MIDDLE SCHOOL ZOMBIE
KING OF THE MUTANTS

Find more books like this at http://www.Month9Books.com

Connect with Month9Books online:
Facebook: www.Facebook.com/Month9Books
Twitter: https://twitter.com/Month9Books
You Tube: www.youtube.com/user/Month9Books
Blog: www.month9booksblog.com

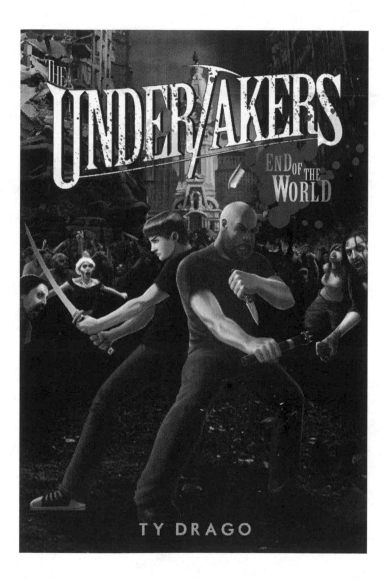

TY DRAGO

KING
of the
MUTANTS
SAMANTHA VERANT